Pr

2

"A simple case ~~t~~
trails that lead back onto themselves. Missing is a book any
mystery lover will enjoy. You won't want to put it down...
Talented Ms. Parker has written a tale that keeps you reading,
wanting to know what happens next. I'll be looking for the
next book in this series. Highly recommended."

–Anne K. Edwards,
Murder and Mayhem Bookclub

"MISSING! Hooked me from page one and never let me go.
To this day I am looking forward to the next K.K. Roarke
Mystery. Parker has a talent for good mystery."

–Alexis Hart,
2001 IPPY Finalist Author

"Ms. Parker has written a very exciting book. There is no
clothesline sag here. The story moves from beginning to end.
It is far too difficult to put this one dawn: you just MUST know
what happened to all these women."

–Shirley Truax,
IvyQuill Reviews

DEADLY DIAMONDS
2003 EPPIE Award Finalist

"DEADLY DIAMONDS is a mystery masterpiece, and Ms.
Parker is the master of the art."

–Sue Hartigan
Reviewers International Organization

"...a Columbo-like investigator...fast paced thriller by Judith
R. Parker. Deadly Diamonds is a four and a half dagger thriller
extraordinaire."

–Evelyn Gale

Judith R. Parker

MISSING!

A K.K. Roarke Mystery

Echelon Press
712 Briarwood Lane
Hurst, Texas 76053

First Echelon Press paperback printing: September 2003
Cover Art © Stacey L. King

Printed in Lavergne, TN, USA

Dedication

For
Donna Miller, who, despite the miles that separate,
has remained a dear and trusted friend
and
Lee Undsderfer, Jo Dereske and Louise Hendricksen, whose
encouragement and support keep me writing
and
most of all, my husband,
who puts up with my fits and starts.

CHAPTER ONE

I was leaning back in my chair, feet propped on my desk, reading a book about Chinese porcelain, and listening to a language tape, when *he* walked in. The tape was supposed to be the sound of waves breaking on a beach covering a subliminal lesson in Chinese, but it sounded like static to me.

I glanced up then took a second, longer look. He was an inch or two over six feet and two hundred pounds of well developed muscle, with curly black hair just touched with gray and the bluest eyes I'd ever seen. White teeth gleamed in a tanned face as his lips twisted into what I guessed was supposed to be a smile. "Roarke Investigations?" he asked. His voice sounded deep, with just the slightest hint of brogue, and it sent a tingle down my spine and into my nether parts. He glanced around the room and back at me.

I tugged off the headphones, dropped the book on the desk, and sat up. "Yes. What can I do for you?"

"I'd like to speak to K. K. Roarke."

My office is on the third floor of an old brick building a couple of blocks from Pioneer Square in downtown Seattle. The sign on the door reads: K. K. Roarke, Investigations.

That's me. Kerry Kathleen Roarke. Girl investigator. Among other things. Just for the record, I'm thirty-three, five feet six with has been politely called a willowy figure. I've been called other things less polite, like string bean and toothpick. I *do* have breasts. Unfortunately they are the size of oranges rather than the proverbial melons. My hair is just a shade too dark to be called carroty, and I wear it short. It has a natural wave, and with a good cut, is definitely wash and wear. I prefer well tailored slacks to jeans, don't carry a gun, and have never killed anyone.

I may not be everyone's idea of a private eye, but I'm good at what I do. Thanks to a trust fund, I only take those cases that interest me. Right now I was interested enough to at least listen to this gorgeous hunk.

I put on my most professional smile. "I'm K. K. Roarke. Won't you sit down? What seems to be the problem?"

He continued to hesitate while his glance roamed uncertainly over me, then the office again, but he pulled the chair closer and dropped his large frame into it. "I want you to find my sister."

At least he wasn't asking me to get the goods on a straying wife. I don't do divorce work. I take a few routine jobs just to keep busy, but I specialize in finding missing persons. Runaways, parental kidnappings, defecting spouses, and even an occasional missing heir. I have personal reasons for detesting deserters, those who run away leaving pain and chaos behind. I get a lot of satisfaction out of my work.

I pulled a legal pad out of a drawer and a copy of my rates and conditions. I tossed the rate sheet across the desk. "Read that. If you're still interested, I'll need you to sign a contract."

He glanced at the sheet, folded it and stuck it in his pocket and pulled out a checkbook. "My name is Ian Donlevy," he said, writing a check. He tore it out and slid it across the desk along with a business card.

I glanced at the card. Donlevy Marine. Custom boats. Ian Donlevy, President. I was impressed, but didn't want to let it show. I'd heard of Donlevy Marine and seen some of their custom designed boats. They were way out of my class but a girl can dream. I turned my attention back to what he was saying.

"My sister's name is Maureen Trent. She left home eleven days ago and hasn't been seen since."

"Okay. Hold on a minute." I pulled out a contract, stuffed it in the typewriter, filled in the blanks, and gave it to him to sign. I find being business-like impresses the clients and increases their confidence in me.

When he'd signed the contract, I handed him his copy and picked up my pen. "Okay. Maureen Trent. Is she married?"

"Yes. To Arthur Trent. He works for me."

"Why do you want to find your sister?" I wondered why he was here and not her husband.

"What do you mean, why? Because she's been missing for eleven days, for God's sake!"

"Are you sure she's missing? Maybe she had a spat with her husband and needs a cooling down period."

He ran a hand through his hair and glared at me. "You sound just like the police."

"Then you have filed a missing person report. What do the police say?"

"They think she just took off. They're really not interested."

"What makes you think she didn't?"

"Take off?" He ran his fingers through his hair again. "She had no reason to do so. She was completely happy. They'd bought a new house just a few months ago and she was still wrapped up in decorating it. Besides, Maureen's not the kind to just walk out on her commitments."

"Okay, let's start at the beginning. How old is Maureen? How long has she been married to–" I glanced down at my notes. "Arthur Trent?"

"She's thirty-two and they've been married for three years." "Any previous marriages?"

"No. She lived with a guy, Mark Kiner, for a while but that was a long time ago. They broke up when he moved back east somewhere."

I added the name to my notes. Probably nothing there, but I'd check it out. "Tell me about the day she disappeared."

He shrugged and his fingers strayed back to his hair. Was it just an unconscious mannerism or was Ian Donlevy more nervous than he appeared? "I can't tell you much. A neighbor, Belle Goodrich, saw her leave the house about eight-thirty on the morning of the nineteenth. She was wearing a red wool suit and carrying her briefcase and purse. No luggage. She drove off and hasn't been seen since."

I glanced at my calendar. The nineteenth was a Friday. "What kind of car was she driving?"

"A white Mustang."

"Did she leave before or after her husband?"

"Arthur wasn't there. He'd left the night before for California to attend a symposium at the University of California and some kind of reunion. That's why no one realized she was missing until Monday."

"Any boyfriends?" A weekend fling while hubby was away was my first thought. Still, eleven days was a long time. Maybe the sex was so good they'd lost track of time.

"Good God, no. Maureen wasn't that kind of person." He glared at me. "If you think she took off with someone, then you're wrong. Maureen wouldn't do that to Arthur."

I didn't say anything, but he must have seen something in my face. He added, "Besides, she was very conscientious. She took her volunteer work with Clean Sweep and Tree Alert

4

seriously. She had several commitments last week."

I'd heard of Tree Alert, a radical environmental group that liked to chain themselves to trees and get involved in other, not so innocuous, activities. Clean Sweep was new to me, so I asked.

Donlevy was back to the hair bit. It was still an appealing gesture, but I wondered how long it would take to become irritating. "I don't know much about Clean Sweep myself. From what Maureen has told me, I gather it's a new group formed to put pressure on the police and city government to get drug dealers and the homeless off the streets or something. They've got an office somewhere in the Central District."

"Did she have a job?"

"No. She quit her job a couple of years ago."

"What kind of work did she do?"

"She was a real estate appraiser for Fiedler-McLaren, the mortgage company. She went to work for them right out of college, took some real estate courses, and worked her way up in the company. She was in line for a vice presidency when she quit."

"Why did she quit?" I was more than a little curious. Not many people who have invested that much time and effort and have climbed that high simply walk out.

"She talked about starting her own business."

"Did she?"

"She had an office fixed up in their house and I think she bought and sold a couple of pieces of property, but as far as I know, that's all."

"I'll need photographs of your sister."

He pulled out his wallet, flipped through it, then tossed a wallet-size studio portrait on the desk. I picked it up and studied it. Maureen was a beautiful woman with the same

5

black hair and blue eyes as her brother, but there was something in her eyes and the way she held her head that detracted from her looks. It was more than mere haughtiness; it was a look of contempt. Was that contempt for the whole world or just the photographer? I turned the picture over and read the stamp on the back. Myron Westover Studios followed by the address.

"Do you have any recent candid shots of your sister?" Studio portraits are okay but they're frequently retouched. For identification, candid shots are better because they usually show more about a person than just the facial features.

"Not with me."

"Why don't you drop a half a dozen or so recent ones in the mail to me?" I asked him a few more questions; vital statistics, hobbies, interests and such and told him I'd get to work right away.

He stood, then hesitated. I waited, but he obviously changed his mind about whatever he was going to say. He shrugged and said he'd be in touch.

As the door closed behind him, I glanced at my watch. Three o'clock. I picked up the phone and called Sam McCready at the Seattle Police Department.

Sam and I have a love/hate relationship. Sam had been the officer-in-charge when a freaked out punk after drug money killed dad. They had never caught the perp and for a year after the killing, Sam had come around every couple of weeks. Even at the grand old age of eleven, it hadn't taken me long to catch on to the fact that all of the questions and mug shots were only an excuse. Sam McCready had a crush on Mom. I don't think Mom has ever caught on. As far as I can tell, she just considers him a good friend.

For nearly a year after Dad was killed, Mom tried to run

the liquor store alone then sold out to a Korean couple. We moved away from the south central district, but that didn't stop Sam from coming around, although not as often. At first I'd hated him for wanting to take Dad's place but as I grew older and came to know him better, I mellowed. Now, I'd be more than pleased if Mom would marry him. She needs a man in her life.

Sam and I had had some bitter words when I went to law school and again when I got my P.I. license. Sam's the kind of guy who believes women belong in the kitchen, or if they must work, then only nursing and teaching are acceptable professions. He thinks lawyers are the scum of the earth, a view I came to share, which is one of the reasons why, although I passed my bar, I've never practiced. Still, he's always helped me when he could. I suppose it's his way of looking out for me. What I wanted from him now was information from the police report. He said he'd look it up and give me a call at home.

I spent the next couple of hours on the phone checking with all of the hospitals. No Maureen Trent and no Jane Doe's matching her description had been admitted at any time since the nineteenth. I even checked the morgue, but they had no unidentified female bodies. I called an old high school buddy who does my computer work for me and asked him to run a check on Maureen.

Francis is a real computer nut and a darned good friend. He's been trying for years, without success, to interest me in computers.

I started a file on the case, writing down all of the information Ian Donlevy had given me. I might sometimes forget something I've heard, but once it's in writing, it's there forever.

When I finished putting my notes in order, I stuck the business card and picture in my wallet, made out a deposit slip for the check, put the file and my cassette player in my briefcase, and shrugged into my coat. The first thing I wanted to do was survey the scene of the disappearance. If Arthur Trent was home, maybe I could check out the inside of the house. I wondered again why Donlevy had come to me instead of Trent.

On the way I stopped by the bank, deposited the check, and collected some cash. I have plenty of plastic but I prefer to use cash whenever possible. Plastic leaves a paper trail, cash doesn't. Maybe I've tracked down too many dead-beat dads and absconding accountants. I only use plastic when I want the copies for billing or taxes.

The Trent home turned out to be a prime piece of real estate on Queen Anne Hill with a view of Puget Sound and the Olympic Peninsula. I parked two doors away and walked back. The house was old but had obviously been remodeled and well maintained. It was two stories, painted white with blue trim and the dormers in the mansard roof indicated an attic. On the left, a concrete driveway led back to a one-car garage attached to the house by a roofed and trellised breezeway. Heavy vines triumphantly waving their new leaves hid the backyard.

There was a postage stamp size front yard filled with rose bushes just beginning to leaf out. Rhododendrons bursting with new blooms nestled against the white lattice that covered the bottom of the porch.

I climbed the steps and paused. If the view from the street had been good, from the porch, it was spectacular. Obviously the Trents weren't hurting in the pocketbook. The size and location of the house, coupled with that view, shouted big, *BIG* bucks.

I would have expected the porch to be furnished with white wicker in keeping with the age of the house. Instead, the chairs were made from white tubular plastic, the kind used for plumbing, and bright blue canvas. A matching blue awning was rolled back against the house. The floor was painted a battleship gray and the tables were polished brass. The whole porch had a nautical air. The guy obviously brought his work home with him. I turned back to the door and hunted for a doorbell. There wasn't one. What appeared to be a ship's bell was mounted head high, on the molding. I couldn't help wondering how many people had bumped their heads on it.

Before I could decide whether to ring the damned thing or just knock, a voice yoo-hooed from somewhere behind me. I looked around but saw no one. I raised my hand to knock and the voice called, "Not home."

I crossed the porch and peered over the railing, but still saw no one. I was about to turn away when the voice spoke again. "He's at work and she's gone."

What I had taken for one of those painted garden gnomes suddenly came to life. Bright eyes peered up at me from under a bamboo coolie hat. Slowly the figure straightened into a tiny old woman dressed in faded blue pedal pushers, something I hadn't seen in years, and a red shirt.

I trotted down the steps and into the next yard. She pulled off a garden glove and extended a hand so small and fragile, I was almost afraid to take it. There was nothing fragile about her grip.

I asked the first thing that popped into my mind. "What do you mean, gone?"

Her eyes, as black as obsidian, peered out of a wrinkled, parchment-dry face that looked like it had just been unwrapped from an Egyptian sarcophagus. She looked at least a hundred years old. Despite her age and clothing, there was an old world elegance about her, and something struck a chord in my memory, but I couldn't place it. "She went away." Her voice was as dry and cracked as her skin and had an intriguing French accent.

"How do you know?"

"I saw her. She came out with an arm load of clothes and dumped them in her car," a look of distaste flashed across her face, "wearing nothing but her night dress. Who are you?"

I pulled out a card and handed it to her. "A relative is worried. I've been hired to find her."

She turned the card over several times, ran a finger over the raised printing, and finally stuck it in her pocket. If it had been a coin, I'm sure she would have bitten it. She didn't seem inclined to continue the conversation so I asked, "You say she was wearing a robe when she left?"

She shook her head. "No robe, just a night gown when I saw her. She didn't leave until later."

"What was she wearing when she left?"

"I don't know. I didn't see her. I just heard the car leave."

"So you don't know whether she was alone or not."

"No, but I suppose she was. He left earlier."

My attention pricked up. This wasn't what she'd told the police. "Her husband?"

"Not him. He went away the night before."

"I'm not quite sure I follow you. Arthur Trent left Thursday night and another man left Friday morning? What did this other man look like?"

She shrugged and started to turn away. "I only saw him from the back and it was still dark."

"How do you know it wasn't Mr. Trent?"

She looked at me over her shoulder. "Because I know Mr.

Trent. He's a nice man. Too nice for the likes of her. This other person was much bigger. Maybe the same height, but bigger." She spread her hands apart. "Big shoulders."

"Why didn't you tell this to the police when they questioned you?"

She stopped and turned back. "I never talked to the police."

"Aren't you Belle Goodrich?"

She drew herself up, and even with her spine as rigid as a steel beam, she didn't reach my shoulder. "I am Simone de la Figoniere. I have nothing more to say to you. Belle Goodrich, indeed." Her voice was colder than the glacier on Mt. Rainier.

She turned and marched regally away, insulted dignity radiating like a force field, leaving me with a dozen half-formed questions dancing though my brain.

CHAPTER TWO

So Maureen Trent did have a boyfriend and she had taken clothes with her when she left. Ian Donlevy wasn't going to be happy about that. I would have liked to ask Mrs. de la Figoniere a few more questions but now was obviously not the time.

The clouds that had been hovering all day were now black and heavy. I glanced at my watch and saw that it was nearly five-thirty. Not much more I could do today. I got in my car and headed home. The traffic on the I-90 bridge across Lake Washington was heavy but then it always is. Not for the first time I considered moving my office to the east side; Bellevue or Kirkland or maybe all the way out to Issaquah. I was getting tired of the forty-mile drive each way, even in my comfortable Lincoln Town Car. Once I'd decided to accept the trust fund, the first thing I'd done was to junk the ratty old clunker I'd drive since high school and buy my dream car. I like big roomy cars, and there's no way I'm going to drive a stick shift. Too much work. Give me comfort and convenience any day.

My mind kept going back to my interview with Simone de la Figoniere. It brought back memories I would rather have forgotten. I knew all too well what it felt like to have someone run out on you, the emptiness, the guilt, the pain, and most of all, the feeling of failure.

The day after I graduated from law school my husband of six months, Tony Proculo, walked out on me with no warning and no explanation. Just a bunch of legal papers with a Post-It note telling me to divorce him for desertion. The legal papers turned out to be an irrevocable trust that would keep me in comfort for the rest of my life.

Tony's desertion shattered me so badly I'd collapsed for several weeks. The trust fund did nothing to ease the hurt and desolation. In fact, at first I thought it was simply a cruel joke. I'd have torn the papers up if my mother hadn't stopped me.

I'd gone to college on scholarships, and I'd supported myself with part-time work as a waitress. The Green Grouse Family Restaurant was where I'd met Tony. Although he was older than me by several years but something about him reminded me of lost, lonely little boy although he was in his thirties. His sad brown eyes drew me immediately. When he started coming in for coffee toward the end of my shift and staying to walk me home, I was touched.

Most of our dates were spent going on long walks or picnics by the lake. Tony was enrolled in the Fine Arts Department. He'd never told me much about himself, only that he hadn't known for a long time what he'd wanted to do with his life. He'd never talked about his family and he'd worked part-time as a bartender. After we were married, we lived in a cheap studio apartment, counted pennies, and concentrated on our studies. I thought we had been happy.

Then he was gone.

By the time I'd pulled myself together, I'd lost the chance to join one of the top law firms, but I no longer cared. Mom was no help. She'd liked Tony and couldn't believe I didn't know why he'd left me. I'm sure she believed, still believes, I'd done something to drive him away. My grief finally turned to anger. I wanted to know why he left. I was determined to find the bastard.

I spent a couple of days at the Public Library reading every book I could find on police procedures and investigative techniques. I have a couple of gifts that helped; I'm a speed reader and I'm blessed, or cursed, with a very good memory. It took me a little over two months to locate Tony, shacked up in Mexico with his lover, a guy named Frank Maldenado.

Tracking Tony down had been a challenge and after the divorce, I went to work for a national detective agency. Most of the work was boring, but when I was assigned to locate a child abducted by her father, I was hooked. I got my P. I. license and opened my own office.

I don't need the money any more but I have this hang-up. I hate to be bored. And the best antidote I've found for boredom is to keep busy. I have a lot of interests but none of them offer the mental challenge of my job. Like I said, I have personal reasons for hating people who run away.

I shook my head, trying to shake loose the past and concentrated on my driving. A light rain was falling by the time I turned off the freeway and onto the winding two-lane road. It was pouring when I reached my drive. I live alone in an old two-story farmhouse on twenty acres in the foothills of the Cascades. Alone, that is, except for two dogs and a white Persian cat. I have plenty of company if I want it, though. My mother lives in a guest house on the property a couple of hundred yards away, and Julio and Carmen Torres live over the garage, a converted barn.

Finding Carmen was a Godsend because I hate housework. I like a clean, well kept house. I just don't want to have to do the work myself. She also makes the most delicious tamales and enchiladas this side of Mexico City and I love Mexican food.

Julio does the yard work and takes care of my horses,

three Tennessee Walkers. I love to ride, but without Julio, I wouldn't be able to keep my own horses. I'm gone too much of the time.

I parked at the side of the house and dashed in the kitchen door. Carmen was seated at the kitchen table, chopping cilantro. She looked up, smiling, when I burst through the door. "*Senor* McCready call. He say he stop by later, he say you owe him dinner. My cousin, Pablo, bring some peppers from Yakima today. Nice and fresh, picked this morning, so I make Chiles Rellenos tonight. Also fresh salsa."

My mouth was already watering. "Great, I'll call Mom."

Wiley, a German shepherd named after Wiley Coyote, and Shybaby, a blue merle Australian sheepdog, met me in the hall with welcoming yaps and waving tails. I stopped to give them both a hug and endure a wet-tongue face wash.

In the den I use for a home office, I tossed my briefcase on the desk and called Mom, inviting her to dinner. Maybe Sam would wangle an invitation out of Mom for after dinner drinks at her place. I never miss a chance to throw them together.

With the dogs traipsing at my heels, I headed upstairs. When I started remodeling the old house, one of the first things I did was tear out walls. I hate small, crowded rooms. The master bedroom and bath take up half the upstairs. The bathroom is huge, with a Jacuzzi in one corner, a tile shower big enough for six, a lavatory with a lighted beauty bar that I seldom use, and the toilet in its own cubicle. At the far end of the room is an exercise area with a Nautilus machine, a Nordic Track, and a television mounted on the wall.

I'm not one of these health nuts. I don't think of my body as a temple or any of that garbage, but in my line of work, staying in shape is a necessity. Besides, I love to cross country ski in the winter and scuba dive in the summer. Both are a lot more fun if I'm in shape.

Someday I may even stop smoking, but not as long as the self-appointed guardians of the nation's health keep trying to force me. My health is my own business. When the factories stop spewing out toxins and the health nuts give up polluting the air with their automobiles, then maybe I'll stop adding my few puffs of cigarette smoke to the atmosphere.

I turned on the Jacuzzi and stripped, stepping around the dogs curled up in the middle of the room, to toss my washables in the hamper and my wool slacks on top for Carmen to send to the cleaners. I took a quick shower and walked, dripping, across to the Jacuzzi. As soon as I stepped into the water, Nefertiti, the cat, hopped up on the rim and began her nightly lecture. She thinks either I am a cat or she is a human. Either way, water is definitely to be avoided. She patrols the rim, scolding, and occasionally hooks me with a paw and tries to pull me out.

The hot water worked its usual miracle, easing away the tension, loosening both muscles and mind. I get some of my best insights while dozing in the Jacuzzi and tonight was no exception. Through half closed eyes, my glance fell on the slacks I'd just taken off. Simone de la Figoniere's words flashed through my mind. An armload of clothes. Not a suitcase—an arm load. Cleaners. Maureen Trent wasn't carrying clothes for a trip. She was going to the cleaners.

When I came downstairs, Mom was in the living room, sipping a glass of wine. I was relieved to see that she was wearing a skirt and sweater. Half the time she shows up in paint smeared jeans. I'd swear she cleans her brushes on the legs on her pants.

When I'd first bought this place, I'd tried to talk Mom in coming to live with me, but she's independent as hell. I'd finally convinced her to leave her scruffy apartment by adding a large studio onto the north side of the guest cottage, a room with plenty on north windows and skylights. Cottage is a misnomer; it's really a lovely two-bedroom house with its own attached garage and shrub enclosed garden. I'd finally convinced her that by moving in and not having to pay rent, her annuity from Dad's insurance would be enough for her to quit work and spend her time doing what she likes best–painting.

"I got a new case today," I announced, crossing to the miniature bar and taking out a red soda can. I'm a coke-a-holic, Coca Cola, that is. I watched Mom out of the corner of my eye as I tossed a handful of ice in a glass and poured the soft drink. I love my mother dearly but we disagree on a lot of things. My work for one. She just can't or won't understand how much satisfaction it gives me. If she had her way, I'd be married, preferably to a 'professional' man, and spend my days cooking and raising a houseful of rug rats. "A man has hired me to find his missing sister. Sounds pretty routine," I added, hoping to stave off a lecture.

I watched her take a deep breath but the doorbell rang before she could get started. I dashed across the room and opened the door. "Saved by the bell," I whispered as I hugged Sam.

Sam McCready isn't much taller than I am but he's big and none of it is fat. He has thick brown hair, beginning to gray, a full beard, and bushy eyebrows. His brown eyes can be soft as a doe's or as hard as a piece of petrified wood. Most of the time he reminds me of a teddy bear.

I led him into the living room, where he greeted Mom with a shy smile. Sam is a tough cop but around my mother he acts like a teenage boy on his first date. And this after twenty years of courting.

Getting a can of beer from the bar, I popped the top and handed it to him. "Sam and I have some business," I told Mom. "I thought we'd go in the den and get it taken care of before dinner."

Mom made a little grimace of distaste but didn't say anything. Sam followed me into the den. I closed the door and asked, "What have you got for me?"

He pulled some papers from his pocket. "This is the police report. You can look it over but I have to have it back."

There wasn't much. The investigating officer had interviewed Arthur Trent and Belle Goodrich. It was basically the same information Ian Donlevy had given me. They'd checked the hospitals and morgues, too, and there was an APB out on Maureen's car. Only three new pieces of information interested me.

Someone at Clean Sweep named Claudia Oliver had been interviewed and confirmed that Maureen had missed an important meeting on Tuesday and another on Thursday of the week after she had disappeared. From the notes, Oliver didn't appear to think it unusual. That contradicted the impression Donlevy had given.

The second item was in the interview with Arthur Trent. He hadn't stayed in a hotel in San Francisco, but with a friend. The name Elliot Brill, together with his address, was listed. However, there was no report of any contact with Brill.

And Arthur Trent hadn't reported his wife missing until ten o'clock in the evening. Had I just assumed he'd reported her missing on Monday morning?

I added both names to my notes and handed the report back to Sam. Leaning back in my chair, I said, "I can add something. I talked with the neighbor on the south, Simone de la Figoniere. She saw Maureen Trent earlier that morning. She also saw a man leave the house. She's certain it wasn't Arthur Trent."

Sam nodded. "The Trent broad's off somewhere having herself a wing-ding. Why not let her enjoy herself?"

"Because my client doesn't believe she ran off. He's paying me to find her. Nothing was said about bringing her back. I don't intend to interrupt a romantic interlude, if that's what it is. I'll leave that up to my client, once I locate her."

"Who are you working for?"

I grinned. "Now, Sam, you know I can't tell you that. Let's see if dinner's ready. I know you didn't drive all the way out here just to bring me this."

Sam's chuckle sounded as deep and rumbling as a volcano about to erupt.

During dinner, Sam kept the conversation centered around art. When he'd first started coming around, Sam hadn't known a Rembrandt from a Donna Payne Miller. Mom studied art before she married my father, and now that she no longer has to work she's taken up painting in a big way. I encouraged Sam to take a couple of courses in art appreciation at the local community college. From the look on his face when I brought it up, you'd have thought I'd suggested he turn himself into a eunuch, but he suffered through them and now he can carry on a reasonably intelligent conversation about art.

Back in the living room, I winked at Sam and said, "Mom, why don't you take Sam over to your place for after dinner drinks. I've got to make some calls and go over my notes."

When they were gone, I headed for the den. I wanted to talk to Arthur Trent. According to the police report, he had no idea where his wife could be. If she was off with a boyfriend, I could believe that. But chances were some friend of hers might know. I needed a list of her closest friends.

Missing!

I looked up the number and called the Trent house hoping to make an appointment for an interview the next day. There was no answer although I let it ring fifteen times.

The police hadn't bothered to check on Trent, but I don't like loose ends. I got the Brill number from information, but all I got when I called was an answering machine. Knowing I'd be out of the office most of the next day, I didn't bother to leave my number, just a message that I'd call again.

I filled out a time sheet I keep on all my cases, typed up a synopsis of the police report and my interview with Simone, and placed them in the file. Then, to help me put my thoughts in order, I made a list of all the avenues I needed to pursue. The police had an APB on the car, so I decided to forget it for the time being. They'd find it a lot faster than I would.

When I finished, I took the dogs for a run and then went to bed, hoping it wouldn't be raining in the morning.

I'm an early riser. I love the fresh clean scent and feel of breaking day. The sun was still hidden behind the Cascades, its first rays painting the high clouds with ribbons of pink and yellow, when I headed for the stable. Julio saw me coming and led out Robin Adair, the gelding I use for hacking. Unless it's pouring rain or snowing, I ride for an hour every morning.

Robin was feeling his Cheerios and we'd been out fifteen minutes or more before he settled into his stride. A Tennessee Walker's gait, besides being as smooth as silk, is as fast as most horses trot. Nothing blows the cobwebs out of my brain and sets me up for the day like a good brisk early morning ride.

By the time we got back, I was feeling on top of the world. Leaving Robin with Julio to cool down, I headed for the house and a quick shower. When I came down, Carmen had breakfast ready. I'm not a coffee and cigarette person. I like three meals a day, starting with a big breakfast. This morning Carmen had fixed chorizo with scrambled eggs, home made flour tortillas, and fresh squeezed orange juice.

After breakfast I collected my briefcase and headed for town. I stuffed the Chinese language tape in the tape deck and listened to static on the drive into town. I'd studied French and Spanish in school and was fluent in both languages. I was determined to learn Chinese and this seemed an easy way. If it worked.

I headed for Queen Anne Hill, wondering if Belle Goodrich was an early riser. She wasn't. She answered the door in an atrociously bright floral robe, a cigarette dangling from her lips. She'd put on makeup with a heavy hand but obviously hadn't gotten around to combing her peroxide-blonde hair. It stood out from her head like a dry dust mop and with about as much style. Her perfume nearly overpowered the aroma of fresh brewed coffee.

I introduced myself, handing her my card. She stuck it in her pocket without looking at it. "What do you want? I told the police everything I know."

"I have just a few questions. I won't take up much of your time. May I come in?"

"I suppose." She let the door swing open and turned away, leaving me to close it. I followed her down the short hall and into the kitchen. She gestured to a chair. "Want some coffee?"

Without waiting for a reply, she poured two cups and shoved a carton of milk and a bowl of sugar cubes towards me, then plopped down in a chair across the table. She stubbed out her cigarette in an already overflowing ashtray. "Well, shoot."

"How well do you know Mrs. Trent?"

She shrugged. "We've chatted a few times, that's about all."

21

"She didn't mention taking a trip to you?"

"Nah, but I'm not surprised she took off. I wouldn't have stayed with a prick like that either."

"You don't like Mr. Trent?"

"What's to like? The guy's a real jerk. I'd have left him a long time ago. No humor. He always had his nose buried in a book or those blueprints he always brings home. According to her, he never wanted to go out and have any fun. But that wasn't what they fought about."

"They fought? Often?"

She fumbled another cigarette out of the package on the table and lit it. "Well, I don't know about that. I only heard them the one time." She glared at me through the smoke. "I wasn't eavesdropping. They were in the backyard and my kitchen window was open."

"What were they fighting about?"

She shrugged. "Something about a baby. I guess she wanted one and he didn't. I really wasn't listening. She ran into the house crying." She puffed a couple of times. "She looked like hell the next morning. I tried to sympathize with her, just being neighborly like, but she got on her high horse and drove away."

"When was this?"

"Oh, three or four weeks before she took off." She squashed the cigarette and stood up. "Look, I gotta go. I've told you all I know."

I thanked her and started to leave. At the door I thought of another question. "You don't know where Mrs. Trent took her dry cleaning, do you?"

Her eyes widened in surprise, then she shook her head. "You might try Four Star Cleaners at the bottom of the hill. It's the closest."

I found the cleaners and went in. It was a small neighborhood business. Even this early in the morning the heat from the steam presses made the place stifling. The man behind the counter had to weigh close to three hundred pounds, and the way the sweat was pouring off his face, I was surprised he hadn't melted away. I handed him my card and explained about Mrs. Trent being missing.

He scrounged under the counter and came up with a shoebox full of sales slips, riffled through them and selected one. "Yeah. M. Trent. One lady's suit, one man's suit, two trousers. Brought in on the nineteenth. That help you any?"

"Do you know what time she left the clothes? Was she alone?"

He shook his head. "Sorry. Can't help you there. Doubt if I'd recognize her if she walked in right now."

"Has it been picked up?"

He dropped the slip back in the box and turned away, wheezing. "Let me check."

I'd noticed the young black girl at the sewing machine in the corner when I came in, then forgotten her. She moved up to the counter and spoke in a soft voice. "Mrs. Trent was here a little before nine in the morning. She was alone when she came in but there was a man waiting for her when she went out."

"Can you describe the man?"

She shook her head. "Not really. I only saw him from the back. He was about five-ten and skinny."

"What was he wearing?'

"Baggy khaki pants and a brown corduroy jacket. He looked like a bum. Probably hitting her up for money."

"Did you notice the color of his hair?"

"No. He was wearing one of the old fashioned caps, the

sort of flat, cloth ones. I gotta get back to work. Mr. Ambrose don't like me talking to the customers. Oh, one other thing. He was a white man."

She scooted back to the sewing machine as Ambrose came shuffling back and said, "Her clothes are still here."

I pointed to my card, lying on the counter. "Would you give me a call if she comes in to pick them up?"

"Yeah, sure." He turned away, dismissing me, and wheezed his way back to the steam press.

Outside, I paused, sucking in the cool air. I felt like I'd just had a sauna bath. I decided my next call would be on Claudia Oliver at Clean Sweep.

Parking is at a premium in downtown Seattle. I rent a space by the month in a lot near my office, so decided to leave my car there and find Clean Sweep on foot. It couldn't be that far away.

I parked, then hesitated. Before I started climbing the steep hills on which downtown Seattle is built, I'd be wise to make sure Ms. Oliver was in. And it wouldn't hurt to check my messages while I was here.

The red light was flashing on my answering machine. The first message was from Mary Sue Krebs, my best friend and part-time secretary, reminding me we had a lunch date and that she'd be by at eleven-thirty. I was glad she'd called because I'd forgotten.

The second message was from my client. His voice, even on the machine, could send a shivery thrill through me but it was his message that sent a cold chill down my spine. Arthur Trent was in the hospital. He'd apparently tried to commit suicide. He had not regained consciousness yet. Donlevy left a number for me to call.

CHAPTER THREE

I listened to the message a second time, then erased the tape and fell into my chair, wondering if I was now going to be looking for a corpse instead of an erring wife. Or, for that matter, was I still on the case at all.

I tried the number he'd left, but there was no answer. I dug out Ian Donlevy's card and dialed his office. The woman who answered told me my client was at Harborview Hospital but that he had left a message for me. He would meet me in my office at eleven.

A glance at my watch showed nine-thirty. I still had time to visit Clean Sweep. My retainer is non-refundable, so I figured I might as well give Donlevy his money's worth of my time. After all, he hadn't fired me, yet.

I trudged up Yesler, then half way up Second Street before I realized I'd forgotten to call. Hopefully, Claudia Oliver would be there. I found the Clean Sweep offices on the third floor of a building that hadn't yet been gentrified. The reception area was dingy, with peeling paint and worn tile. Half a dozen cheap plastic chairs lined the wall to the right of the door. The wooden desk looked like Army surplus, circa World War Two.

The woman behind the desk would have dwarfed George Foreman. I squashed down the impulse to leave the door open for a quick getaway. I wasn't entirely relieved when she smiled. Her teeth, gleaming a brilliant white in her dark face, reminded me of the wolf in Little Red Riding hood. Her skin was not just dark, it was black. Not only was she big and black, she was startlingly beautiful. I could picture her, a hundred years in the past, as a warrior queen leading her village into battle.

I approached the desk cautiously and handed her my card. The smile disappeared and she took her time studying it. Finally, she laid it carefully on the desk and asked, "What is this about?" Her voice sounded surprisingly soft and melodious.

"Maureen Trent. I understand she was a member of your group. I was hoping you could tell me a little about her work here. Are you Claudia Oliver?"

"No. Claudia is a volunteer. She's only here when she can be spared from her regular job. I'm Angela Bottoms. Claudia told me the police were here asking questions. There's not much more I can tell you."

"How long has Mrs. Trent been a member?"

"We've only been organized for three months. Mrs. Trent was one of our first volunteers."

"How did she become interested? To tell you the truth, I'd never heard of your group until yesterday. You're trying to get drug dealers off the streets?"

"That's one of our goals but it's not at the top of the agenda. First we want to force the city and the state to do something for the homeless." Her eyes lit up and her voice took on enthusiasm. "Do you realize that over half of the homeless are mentally ill? When the mental hospitals closed, these people were just dumped on the street to fend for themselves. They need care and treatment, not thrown in jail for a few days, then back on the street."

I was intrigued in spite of myself. "You're advocating

more mental hospitals?" I'd seen *The Snake Pit* with Olivia de Havilland as a child and it had given me nightmares for months.

"Not necessarily. Only a small percentage actually need institutionalization. What we want are supervised group homes. Here, let me give you some of our literature." She picked up a selection of pamphlets and handed them to me.

"Thanks. I'll read these." I would, too. I might live in the country, but I was exposed to the homeless every day. They congregate on the streets near my office. But I wasn't here to talk about the homeless and said so. "What can you tell me about Maureen Trent?"

"I don't know her well. She gave us a large donation and she came by twice a week for our organizational meetings. Some of her ideas were good but some, well, they were a little extreme. We're not a militant group. We'd prefer to work within the system. To be honest, I'm not sure she would have been with us for long. I suppose I shouldn't say this, but she seemed more interested in taking on the system than in helping the homeless. Perhaps you should talk to Mr. Penman."

"Who is he?"

"Anson Penman. He's an attorney who donates his services. He brought Mrs. Trent to us."

"Where can I find him?"

She gave me his office address and phone number. I told her I would still like to talk to Claudia Oliver and would call for an appointment, thanked her and left. I thought over what Angela had told me on the walk back to my office. My mental picture of Maureen Trent was growing. I wasn't sure I liked what was beginning to emerge.

Ian Donlevy was pacing the hall in front of my office when I got back. There was no smile in his eyes today; they were as cold and stormy as the Barents Sea. He followed me into the office, practically stepping on my heels.

I circled around my desk, wanting something solid between us. I wasn't exactly scared, but he's a big man and there was a leashed violence about him that made me uneasy.

He glared at me for a moment then began to pace. "You got my message?"

I nodded. "Want to give me the details?"

"No!" He barked the word and strode to the door. He stopped, hand on the knob. He didn't open it. Instead, some of the tension drained out of his shoulders and turned back. "I'm sorry. I had no call to yell at you. Jesus, this is driving me crazy. Maureen and now Arthur."

He crossed back to the client chair and threw himself into it, the fingers of his right hand straying to his hair. His left hand clutched the edge of my desk. He stared at his hand, eyes unfocused. "I found him, you know." He stopped playing with his hair and rubbed his eyes. "Arthur hasn't been himself since Maureen disappeared. He didn't show up at the office yesterday and when he didn't come in this morning... I was worried about him. I wanted to tell him about hiring you. I...I thought it might help, knowing someone was doing something. He wasn't downstairs. I called but he didn't answer. I thought maybe he was asleep so I went upstairs. His car was in the garage so I knew he was home."

He paused. When he continued, his voice was barely more than a whisper. "He's been remodeling the attic into a home office. It isn't finished yet. I found him there."

Ian stopped speaking and a tear trickled down his cheek. I waited, knowing he had more to say.

He wiped roughly at the tears and looked at me. "He was hanging from one of the rafters. He must have done it just minutes before I arrived. His face was blue and his tongue... . Oh, God, I'll never forget it as long as I live. I got him down and started CPR. When he was breathing on his own, I called 911. He's in intensive care."

I didn't know what to say. I'm not much good at expressing sympathy. I reached across the desk and laid my hand over his.

After a moment he shook himself, much like a dog does, and straightened, pulling his hand from under mine. I could see that giving way to his emotions embarrassed him.

"Did he leave a note?" I asked, trying to make my voice convey understanding while bringing him back to business.

It seemed to work. He tried a weak smile that didn't quite come off. "Sorry. No. At least if he did I didn't see one. The police are at the house now. Maybe they found one." Taking a deep breath, he asked, "What have you found out?"

I gave him an expunged version of my conversation with Simone de la Figoniere, omitting any mention of the man she'd seen leaving. I figured he'd had enough shocks for one day. It would be in my written report, he could read it then. I told him what I'd learned at the cleaners. I had to ask, "Could that man have been Arthur?"

"No. I suppose you could say Arthur is skinny but he's taller than I am. Besides, he was in San Francisco."

"We only have his word for that."

"Surely the police checked."

I shook my head. "I've read the police report. He told them he was staying with a friend but they never called to check."

"You think he killed her." It was a statement rather than a question. He glared at me.

I shrugged. Statistics show most homicides are committed

by someone close to the victim but that wasn't something my client wanted to hear.

He stood up and began to pace again. "That's what the police think. I don't believe it. It's simply impossible. Arthur loved Maureen. He'd never kill her. No. I won't believe it. There has to be some other explanation for him doing... doing what he did."

He stopped pacing and leaned over my desk. "Find her. Find Maureen and clear Arthur." I was surprised, and I suppose it showed, for he continued, "Arthur is not only an employee and my best power boat designer, he's a good friend. You don't know him. Arthur could never harm anyone. He's one of the gentlest people you'll ever meet. He's simply not capable of violence of any kind."

That's what people said about Ted Bundy but I kept the thought to myself. "I need more information. I had planned to interview Mr. Trent today. Will that be possible?"

He shook his head. "He's in a coma. His neck wasn't broken, he'd strangled. The doctor's don't know if there is brain damage or not but his vocal cords... . Oh, shit. He may never be able to talk normally even if–"

"Then you'll have to tell me. Did Maureen have any close friends? Anyone she might have confided in?"

"Not really. Maureen had lots of acquaintances but no close friends. She was a very private person." He paused, then said, "She did have one friend from college. Connie Phillips might be able to help you."

He took out a pocket appointment calendar, flipped through the address portion in the back, and gave me Connie's address. Almost as an after thought, handed me four snapshots of Maureen. "I'm depending on you to find her. Let me know if you need more money."

"A couple of questions. Was Trent's trip planned in advance or a spur of the moment decision?"

"Oh, it was planned. Arthur told me about it a month or so ago."

"Who else knew about the trip?"

Ian shrugged. "Almost anyone. There was quite a write-up in a trade journal that listed some of the designers attending, including Arthur. There was even a short blurb in the Seattle Times."

"Why didn't your sister go with him?"

He ran his fingers through his hair again. "I don't know. It wasn't something that would have interested her."

"Did she resent his going?"

"I doubt it. He wasn't going to be gone that long."

When he left I studied the pictures. One thing hit me right away. In not one of the photos was Maureen Trent smiling. Two were obviously taken at an outdoor party. Everyone else seemed to be laughing and having a good time but Maureen stood aloof, condescending.

In one picture, a tall, lean man presided over the barbecue. I peered closer, studying the face. It, too, was long and lean. It was a gentle face. He was smiling but there was a haunting sadness in his eyes. I'd seen that look before, in the eyes of survivors of tragedies. Ian Donlevy was right. Arthur Trent didn't look like a killer. But then how many do?

The other two photos had been taken on a boat under sail. They were action shots. I've sailed enough to recognize that Maureen was no novice at crewing and she appeared lithe and athletic. She'd obviously kept herself in shape. In these photos she was more relaxed, obviously enjoying herself, but still no smile. I put the photos in my briefcase.

I sat for a few minutes, running a pencil absently through

my fingers. My gut told me that Maureen was dead. Had Arthur killed her? Why? Was she having an affair? Simone's story indicated it was likely. Had Arthur found out? What was the significance of the baby conversation Belle had overheard? Was Maureen pregnant? If so, by whom?

Mary Sue interrupted my musings. She blew into my office like a miniature tornado. "Hey, why the solemn look? Come on, doll, it's lunch time." She strode across the room in the exaggerated stride of a runway model, whirled around, and struck a pose. "How do you like my new rags? I found the darlingest new boutique."

Mary Sue is everything I'm not. She's dainty and feminine, with natural blonde hair and wide blue eyes, the picture of innocence, and a southern accent that thirty years in the Northwest hasn't completely eliminated. We've been friends since high school. Mary Sue is the only person I've ever told the truth about Tony.

During my investigation, I'd learned a few things about my husband that came as a surprise. Like he was a member of a prominent and very respectable eastern family that would take serious exception to his sexual proclivities. Very serious, indeed, and I didn't hate him enough to want to see him alienated from his family. In fact, by the time Tony had poured out his heart to me, I felt more pity than anger. We got a quiet divorce in Mexico and I took back my maiden name.

Tony insisted on the trust fund that keeps me in very comfortable style. I suppose the righteous would say I should have spurned the money but I'm not that righteous or that stupid. If it eased Tony's conscience to provide for me, who was I to argue? I might not have had much time invested in Tony, but he sure as hell had caused me a lot of emotional pain and suffering. I'd truly loved him.

Tony Proculo was everything I'd ever wanted or dreamed of in a husband. He wasn't all that great in bed but then there are a lot of qualities more important to a lasting relationship than just sex. Things like kindness and sensitivity, empathy, patience, dependability and honesty. Tony had it all—except the last two. I had not only loved Tony but I had liked him. I still do.

In fact, we're now almost friends, but I've never quite trusted another man enough to legally commit myself. Which is not to say that I don't enjoy their company from time to time.

Mom is always after me to "find a good man and settle down," but Mary Sue understands. She's been through a rough divorce and claims she now prefers to play the field. There's a lot of steel under that flighty exterior. She's the only person I completely trust.

She tapped a foot impatiently. "Come on, Kerry. I'm simply starving."

"Let me make a couple of calls and we can go."

"You've got a new case. Great!"

I dialed the number for Anson Penman but got a busy signal. Then I tried Connie Phillips. She answered on the third ring. I made an appointment to see her at three-thirty, then tried Penman again. His secretary informed me that Mr. Penman was out of town and wouldn't return until Thursday.

Mary Sue kept up a light chatter all through lunch. I listened with half an ear, my mind on Arthur and Maureen Trent. Had Arthur killed his wife and hung himself in a fit of remorse? It was the most logical answer. How well did Ian really know Arthur, or for that matter his sister? Who else would want to kill her? Her lover? What if she was pregnant and not by her husband?

Over coffee, Mary Sue complained, "Kerry, you haven't

heard a word I've said!"

"Sure I have. You've been raving about some guy you met at your health club."

She gave me a disgusted look. "I stopped talking about him ten minutes ago. I asked if we're still on for tomorrow night?"

I looked at her, trying to remember what we'd planned.

She gave me an irritated look. "The exhibit of Chinese porcelain. How could you forget? It was your idea."

Damn. I had been looking forward to visiting the traveling exhibit. Ancient Chinese porcelain is one of my passions. So far I've only collected two pieces, a bottle vase from the K'ang Hsi period and a footed bowl with a pointed convex base of luminous white porcelain from the Yung Cheng dynasty. Both are museum quality. I shook my head regretfully. "I'd better pass. I don't know how tied up I'm going to be."

"So what's your new case?"

I gave her a quick rundown. After all, she would learn about it soon enough. She types up all my cases and does my billing.

It was almost two o'clock when we parted. I walked back to my car. It was too early for my meeting with Connie Phillips but there was someone else I wanted to see. I took out the studio portrait and studied it again, then turned it over. According to the address stamped on the back, the Westover Studio was located in a strip mall on Aurora Avenue.

I eased through the downtown traffic and headed north on Aurora Avenue past the cheap motels, pawnshops, auto parts stores. I love Aurora Avenue. Anything you want, and I do mean anything, can be found somewhere on the street.

I passed the remnants of Aurora Village, one of the oldest

shopping malls in Seattle. I hated to see it go. Although it was one of the oldest malls in the northwest, it had always been my favorite.

I found the strip mall but all of the parking spaces were taken and I had to park several blocks away and walk a jillion miles before I found the studio. It was tucked away in one of the smaller spaces. Only one photograph was on display in the window, a photograph of a teenage girl and Myron Westover had caught that ephemeral moment of half girl, half woman, not just in the features but in the pose. He'd captured all of the innocent wonder of the child, the adolescent yearnings and still shown the woman she would become. It was a remarkable photograph. I had to tear myself away.

Inside, the reception area was small. An antique spindle-legged table flanked by two velvet chairs were grouped in the corner on my right. A young woman manned the small desk on the left. I recognized her instantly from the photograph in the window. She was older but the promise of the photograph had been realized. The nameplate on desk simply identified her as Alice. I wondered if she was Westover's daughter.

I handed her my card and asked to see Myron Westover.

She glanced at the appointment book open on the desk and gave me a doubtful look. "Do you have an appointment?"

I smiled my most charming smile. "No. I'm not here for a sitting. I need to talk to him about a portrait of someone else. I really only need a minute of his time."

"He has a sitting in fifteen minutes."

"I doubt if it will take that long."

She hesitated a moment, then asked me to have a seat and disappeared through a door to the back. Before I had a chance to sit down, she popped her head back in. "Come this way." She led me down a short hall, past two closed doors, one on each side, and into the studio, then retreated to the reception room.

Myron Westover wasn't at all what I'd expected. He was a short, rotund little man with a balding head he tried to disguise with strands of hair combed forward. Wide blue eyes danced in a round, baby smooth face. He had to be in his fifties but looked much younger, perhaps because he seemed to vibrate with energy.

I pulled out the portrait of Maureen and handed it to him. "I'm hoping you can tell me something about one of your clients.

He glanced at the picture, then back at me. His eyes were no longer smiling. "Maureen Donlevy." He almost hissed the name as he tossed the picture back. "Who are you?"

I gestured to the card he was holding. "I'm a private detective. Do you know her? Personally, I mean?"

"What's she done now?"

"Nothing that I know of. She's missing. I've been hired to find her. What can you tell me about her?"

"She's a grade A bitch." He paused. "Missing, huh? Probably tried to con the wrong person. Who hired you?"

"I can't tell you that."

"Some other sucker she's conned? Well, I hope you find her. The bitch deserves to get what coming to her."

He had more to say. I could see it building in him. I waited. Finally, he sighed and said, "Come on in my office."

I followed him back into the hall and through one of the doors. He shoved a mess of proof sheets into a pile at the end of a love seat, making room for me to sit, then settled behind his cluttered desk. "Okay, what do you want to know?"

"When did you first meet Maureen?"

"About six years ago. She came in with one of my clients

to pick up some pictures. Mark saw her and fell for her in a big way."

The name rang a bell and it took me only a moment to place it. "Mark Kiner?"

His eyebrows shot up. "You know about Mark?"

"Her brother told me they had lived together. That's all."

"Yes? Did he tell you that Mark loved the bitch, wanted to marry her? No, I can see he didn't." He pulled a handkerchief from his back pocket and mopped his forehead. "She moved in with him for a few months. Trial marriage, she called it. Insisted they share everything, joint credit, joint bank account. Oh, she was smooth, all right. Two months after she moved in, Mark turned twenty-five and came into his inheritance. It wasn't all that much. About forty thousand in cash and some Boeing stock worth another fifty. And the house, of course."

He mopped his brow again. "She talked him into selling the stock. Had him convinced they could use the money to go into business together. Sold him some hogwash about buying an old motel down the coast and turning it into a big resort. Wanted him to sell the house, too, but he wouldn't do that. She worked on him for several months but when he wouldn't budge, she cleaned out the accounts and walked."

"Did Mark get his money back?"

"Hell, no. He didn't even try. The money was the least of it, as far as Mark was concerned. He really loved the bitch and her leaving tore him apart."

"I understood they broke up when he moved back east."

Myron Westover didn't answer for a moment. He played with a paper knife, caressing it with his fingertips and something about the way he handled it sent a chill racing up my spine. When he looked up, his eyes blazed with hatred.

His voice was bitter as he answered. "Mark didn't move back east, just east of the mountains. He had a nervous breakdown. He's been in and out of a private hospital for the last five years."

"How do you know all this?"

His eyebrows shot up. "You don't know? Mark is my nephew. Alice's brother." He leaned forward still caressing the knife, eyes glittering. "Maybe she's not missing. Maybe she's got herself killed." He chuckled and leaned back, dropping the paper knife on the desk. "If someone's killed the bitch, then it's good riddance."

CHAPTER FOUR

Walking back to my car, I wondered how many other people Maureen had cheated. How many other people had reason to hate her? I also wondered how much Ian Donlevy really knew about his sister. Myron Westover had reluctantly given me the name and address of the hospital where Mark was a patient. It was a private substance abuse institution that provided both standard detox programs and long term care. He swore Mark could not have been in town when Maureen disappeared but it was something I wanted to check out for myself.

I headed north for Lynnwood. It took me a while to find the Phillips house. It was a two story white clapboard with a wide porch, set on a deep, triple-sized lot with several fruit trees in the front yard. The farmhouse had been built back in the twenties when the area was still small farms. It looked out of place now, dwarfed by apartment buildings and modern, featureless houses.

The gravel of the long, flower-lined driveway crunched under my tires. Someone was into gardening. The soil under the row of roses had recently been cultivated. Past the house I saw where a large patch of ground had been worked up, ready for spring planting. A little early, in my opinion, but then I'm not a gardener. Beneath a haphazardly thrown plastic tarp I could see a rototiller and a wooden garden cart.

I parked and took a minute to study the house. From the

street, it had looked quaint and attractive. A closer look showed neglect not visible from the street. The paint was chipped and peeling, the porch roof sagged in the center where a post had broken off, the front steps were splintered in places, and the left railing tilted at a crazy angle.

The front door opened as I got out of my car. A woman I assumed to be Connie Phillips waited for me on the porch that stretched across the front of the house. I studied her as I carefully climbed the old wooden steps.

She was a mousy little thing, so slight a good wind would blow her away, with dull brown hair pulled back from her face and held at the nape of her neck with a brown plastic barrette. She was wearing a faded cotton shirtwaist dress and a drab green sweater, anklets and once-white Keds on her feet. She was the complete opposite of what I would have expected the "best friend" of Maureen Trent to be.

"Miss Roarke? I thought we could talk here if you don't mind. Mother is still sleeping." She gestured towards a couple of green painted metal chairs, spotted with rust and damp with condensation.

I sat down gingerly. She settled in the other chair, not seeming to notice the damp and the cold, sitting patiently, hands clasped tightly in her lap.

"I understand that you are a close friend of Maureen Trent. Did you know that she is missing?"

She nodded. "Arthur called me last week."

"Do you have any idea where she might have gone?"

She shook her head. Her glance flitted over the yard and finally settled on her hands.

"Did she talk to you about going away? Mention any plans to take a trip?"

"No."

Her hands had balled into fists. I tried to put her at ease by asking her to tell how she and Maureen had met.

She answered in a flat, little girl voice that grated like a fingernail on chalkboard. "At the University of Washington. We were both taking business courses. She was so beautiful and popular. Sometimes I still can't believe she picked me for a friend. I...I don't make friends easily. Maureen was my first close friend. It was like a miracle. I mean, she had money and looks and everything. And then, in our sophomore year, she asked me to share an apartment with her."

Her fingers began to uncurl. "I was living at home because it was all Mother could do to pay my tuition. She had to mortgage this place just to pay that. I couldn't afford the dormitory or an apartment, but Maureen really wanted me to come, actually begged me."

I felt my eyebrows shooting up. Somehow I couldn't imagine Maureen Trent begging anyone for anything. Connie must have seen my skepticism.

"She did. She said she needed me. Said I could keep the place clean and take care of her clothes and things in exchange for my share of the rent." Her voice hardened. "She did need me."

I glanced at her sharply.

She saw the look, and her lips tightened for a moment. "You wouldn't understand. You're pretty. You don't know what it's like..."

Her voice softened and her eyes took on a dreamy look as she continued. "Maureen was wonderful. It was like I'd always dreamed college would be, like in the movies. Lots of parties and people always in and out. It was...like...like a...whole new world...miraculous...marvelous. We even double-dated. I'd...I'd never had a date, not in high school or

41

college, not until I moved in Maureen. She was so good to me."

Connie's eyes were glowing with an adoration that sickened me. I ground my teeth to keep from uttering my thoughts. *Good to her! Why not, she was getting an unpaid, live-in maid and someone to palm off her unwanted dates on.* I'd be willing to bet she'd only fixed Connie up with nerds, men she didn't want.

I had to look away as Connie continued her eulogy. "Maureen was smart, too, but she was always so busy. Sometimes, I'd even help her write her papers. She used to say she'd never have made it through college if it hadn't been for me."

I gritted my teeth to hold back a sharp retort, then forced the muscles of my jaws to relax, took a deep breath and asked, "How about after college? Did you see much of each other?"

"Oh, yes. When I was working at the bank, before Mother got sick, we would meet for lunch two or three times a month."

"Did she invite you to these luncheons?" I asked, already knowing the answer.

Her smile faltered a little and her answer was tinged with defiance. "Maureen appreciated my calling her. She said she did! She said she looked forward to our lunches, that it was the only time she could really relax, that I was the only person that didn't want something from her. People were always taking advantage of her and she was too kind to say no."

"Who paid for the lunches?"

"I did and I was happy to do so. Maureen had done so much for me."

"What about while she was living with Mark Kiner?"

Something flashed in Connie's eyes and her voice faltered. "No."

"Why not?"

"Mark didn't like her seeing other people. He was terribly jealous and possessive. It made her miserable. That's why she had to leave him. It broke her heart. She really loved him, but he became abusive. She had to leave"

I couldn't help asking, "Weren't you upset that she dropped you?"

She lowered her head and didn't say anything for a moment, just sat twisting her hands in her lap. Finally, she said, "Yes. I didn't see her for quite a while. I thought maybe something I had said or done had driven her away. It was awful."

Tears started trickling down her cheeks but when she looked up, she was smiling again. "But when she came back and explained, I understood. She said I reminded her of the pain and she just hurt too much, she needed time alone to heal. But she said she couldn't stay away, that I was her one true friend.

"For weeks afterward, she'd come out and we'd sit in the car and she'd cry her eyes out. You see, she kept hoping he'd change. Instead, he moved back east somewhere."

"Did she say where he'd moved to?"

"No. I don't think she knew. Just someplace back east."

"What happened then?"

"Oh, it was just like it used to be. Except by then Mother was sick and I'd quit my job so we didn't meet for lunch. Instead, Maureen would come out here. She was so kind and understanding. Sometimes she'd even bring baskets of fruit and things to tempt Mother's appetite."

"What about after she married Arthur Trent?"

"At first, she didn't come very often but she'd call a couple of times a month. She didn't want me to think she'd forgotten me."

"What about Arthur? Do you like him?"

She was back to twisting her fingers and there was a wistfulness in her voice. "I did at first. He seemed such a sensitive man, so thoughtful and gentle." Her voice roughened. "But he was just like all the rest. Selfish and cruel."

"I understand Maureen wanted children but that he refused. Is that what you mean by selfish?"

She looked up. "Oh, no! He was the one that demanded children. He wouldn't understand how frightened Maureen was. You see, the doctor told her..." she looked away, blushing..."she was too small...down there. She was likely to die if she tried to have a baby."

"He knew this?"

"Maureen told him but he didn't believe her. He said cruel things to her."

"Were you there? Did you hear?"

"Oh, no. Maureen told me. She sat right there where you're sitting and told me all about it. She always talked to me. She trusted me, just as I trusted her."

Her expression shifted, but as I could only see her profile, I wasn't sure what it meant.

"I trusted her."

There was something about her voice that bothered me, something just a hair off key. But then I'd never had much patience with adolescent hero-worship. "She talked to you about her marriage?"

"Oh, yes. I couldn't believe he could be so cruel."

"Did you see much of the Trents, together, I mean? Did you visit them?"

"The first year Maureen invited me to dinner several times." Her voice dwindled away and she moved restlessly in the chair.

I pressed. "After that?"

She shook her head. "Maureen said Arthur was too busy to entertain."

Something here didn't ring true. "Did you believe her?"

Her head came up. "Of course. Maureen would never lie to me. She told me everything. She trusted me and I trusted her. We loved each other." She blushed furiously and looked away. "Like sisters, I mean. Not... not–"

Her embarrassment embarrassed me and I asked, "When was the last time you saw her?"

Connie kept her gaze fixed on one of the fruit trees, but she answered quickly, "The week before she left. She brought grapes and pears for Mother. With all her problems, she still thought of Mother. Wasn't that sweet of her?"

"Very. What kind of mood was she in?"

"Kind of nervous and excited at the same time. She wouldn't come in and kept watching the street. She said she'd worked out her problems with Arthur and everything was going to be okay. She didn't stay long."

"Did she say how she'd worked out her problems?"

Connie shook her head. "No, just that everything was going to work out. She was in a hurry. She said she'd tell me all about it later."

"That was all?"

She started to nod, then stopped. "She did say Mark was back and was following her."

I sat up with a jerk. "What!"

"She laughed about it. Thought it was a good joke, that he'd come back after she'd gotten over him. Said it served him right that she'd married someone else." She cocked her head to one side, listening, then sprang up. "Mother's awake. I have to go."

It was raining again, a fine, misty Seattle rain as I got back in my car and headed for highway 405 that would take me south along the east side of Lake Washington. The traffic was heavy and I had to concentrate on my driving until I exited onto I-90. Within a few miles, the traffic thinned and my thoughts centered on Maureen Trent. The more I learned about her, the less I liked her. And I didn't like where I was afraid this case was going.

Maureen used and discarded people. Was that how she planned to solve her problems with Arthur? Was she planning to strip him clean as she had Mark Kiner, then leave him? Had she already lined up another sucker? Did Arthur know? Was Connie Phillips as naive as she appeared? Was it puppy love or something deeper that kept her a willing victim? She appeared a pathetic creature but somehow I didn't feel sorry for her. In fact, I didn't like her at all.

It was dark by the time I got home but I needed to clear my brain. I changed into cords and Reeboks and called the dogs. I know the trails around my place like the back of my hand and the dark doesn't bother me. I took the dogs for a long walk. The things I'd learned about Maureen left me feeling unclean. I let the fine mist and cool, pungent air wash all thoughts of the case from my mind.

Back at the house, I wiped down the dogs' paws, climbed the stairs, and stripped out of my damp clothes. I glanced at the Nautilus but decided I just wasn't up to it this evening. I slipped a ski tape in the VCR and turned on the TV that sits in front of the NordicTrack. I like to pretend I'm skiing along with people on the tape; it makes it seem less like work, and I love the free feeling of skiing naked. I did my twenty minutes, showered off the sweat, and hopped in the Jacuzzi. Tonight there was no mind magic but at least I was physically relaxed when I got out and slipped into a pair of satin lounging pajamas.

Carmen had left a taco casserole in the oven. I heated it, opened a can of Coca Cola, and carried them into the living room. I caught the tail end of the news as I ate, watched a local magazine program, then switched off and headed for the den.

From the information operator, I got the telephone number for the hospital where Mark Kiner was a patient and called. Not surprisingly, they refused to give me any information. I asked for the Director but he was gone for the day. I hung up, waited a few minutes, and dialed again. Lowering the tone of my voice and adding an accent, I asked to speak to Mark Kiner. The phone rang several times before the operator came on to tell me Mr. Kiner must be out of his room. At least I learned he was currently a patient.

I added my notes on the day's conversations to the file and popped it back in my briefcase. I lit a cigarette and leaned back in my chair. I was learning a lot about Maureen Trent but none of it was bringing me any closer to finding her.

The shrill ring of the telephone brought me out of my reverie. I sat up, grabbed the receiver, and muttered hello. Ian Donlevy's voice crackled over the line, choked and sputtering so that I could hardly understand him.

"Slow down and start again," I ordered.

The line went silent for a moment, then I heard him exhale a deep breath. "They have a police guard on Arthur's door. I talked to a detective. They think he killed Maureen."

My throat tightened and my gut began to churn. "Have they found her body?"

"No."

"Then why do they think she's dead?"

"Apparently Arthur did leave a note. On his office computer."

My gut tightened even further. "He admitted killing her?"

"No. The note was to me. It just said, he was sorry but this time it was just too much."

"He said nothing about your sister?"

"No."

"Then why do they think it was a suicide note or that he killed her?"

"They talked to that other neighbor, the ballerina. Why didn't you tell me a man was seen leaving her house that morning?"

A cog slipped in my memory. Ballerina. Of course, Simone de la Figoniere had been a famous premiere danseuse. Mom had taken me to see her years before, when I'd been an impressionable child. For months afterwards I'd dreamed of becoming a ballerina.

Ian's voice brought me back to the present.

"What?"

"I said, why didn't you tell me?"

"Because you were so upset. I didn't want to add to your pain until I could check it out. It would have been in my written report. The police haven't found Maureen's body?"

"No. They think Arthur hid it somewhere."

"And what do you think?"

"Oh, God. I don't know what to think. Arthur is my friend but Maureen is my sister."

"How long have you known Mr. Trent?"

"Since he came to Seattle nine years ago."

"What about his background, where did he come from, where is his family?"

He was silent for a long time. "I thought I knew him well but..."

"What about his references."

"Oh, they're all in order. I checked those thoroughly. He's a graduate of the University of California, Berkeley. Prior to moving to Washington, he worked for Consolidated Marine in Long Beach. They gave him a great recommendation."

"What about personal information?"

"I remember him telling me that his mother died when he was a youngster. His father died about six years ago. He took a week off for the funeral and to take care of things. I got the impression he was an only child, at least he never mentioned any brothers or sisters." I could hear the frustration in his voice.

"Friends, relatives?"

"I don't know. Arthur is a friendly guy but not terribly social, if you know what I mean. He never talked about himself."

"Do you want me to check out Arthur's alibi? I'd have to fly down to San Francisco."

There was a long pause. If I hadn't heard his breathing, I'd have thought we'd been disconnected. When he spoke again his voice was so low I had to strain to hear the words. "It's been just the two of us for so many years. Maureen was only sixteen when we lost our parents. I've tried to take care of her but she's always been so independent."

There was another pause, then he continued, "I introduced them. I thought Arthur would be good for her, give her the security she needed. I encouraged their marriage. I can't believe I could have been so wrong."

He stopped speaking. I waited, feeling his pain, wishing I could say something to comfort him. Finally he spoke again, his voice stronger, more decisive. "Yes. Check Arthur out. Check him out all the way. I've got to know." He hung up before I could answer.

CHAPTER FIVE

I replaced the receiver, then picked it up again, and called Alaska Airlines. If the police thought Arthur Trent had killed his wife, they'd want to question Elliot Brill. I wanted to talk to him first, and I preferred to do it face to face.

I booked a seat on a flight leaving for San Francisco in just over two hours. Hurriedly, I roughed out a report, called Mary Sue and left a message on her answering machine to stop by, type it up and mail it to Ian Donlevy. I scribbled a note to Carmen that I was going out of town and stuck it on the refrigerator door.

Upstairs I scrambled into a beige wool pantsuit, a pair of Easy Spirit pumps in case I had to do more walking than I care to do, and grabbed a lightweight raincoat. San Francisco's fog can be just a damp as Seattle's rain. I threw a couple of changes of clothes, night gear, and lingerie into a carry-on bag, just in case. In the den, I grabbed my briefcase, checked the money in my wallet, made sure I had my credit cards and hurried out to the car. I made my flight with only minutes to spare.

I'd picked up a paperback book by Washington author Louise Hendricksen at the newsstand. The back cover blurb had indicated it contained enough terror to keep me engrossed during the flight. I hadn't quite finished it when the stewardess announced our imminent arrival is San Francisco.

Midweek hotel rooms are not easy to come by in San

Francisco. There was a Revere Hotel van dropping off a passenger so I climbed aboard. If they didn't have a room, at least I'd be downtown. I lucked out; they'd had a no-show. It gripes the hell out of me to pay two hundred dollars for a bed for a few hours, even if it is someone else's money, but I didn't feel like traipsing around town in the middle of the night looking for something less expensive. It's not that I'm exactly cheap; I just like value for my money.

It was an attractive room, but still not worth that kind of dough and I wondered again where hotels find those Munchkin size pillows. It was too late to call Elliot Brill, so I left a wake-up call for six A.M. and crawled in bed.

When the phone woke me, I did a few exercises and went for a brisk walk before trying Elliot Brill. He might not like the early morning as much as I did and there was no sense irritating him. Brill still sounded half asleep when I called at eight o'clock. I didn't want to say too much on the telephone so I simply told him I was in San Francisco on behalf of Arthur Trent and needed to talk to him as soon as possible. He agreed to meet me for breakfast and named a restaurant near the Embarcadero.

With time to spare, I decided to take the cable car. I've never been able to come to San Francisco without taking a ride on one. I love them. We used to have a few in Seattle, before my time, and I've always resented their loss. Sometimes I don't think much of "progress." Lord knows we have the hills and the tourists would love them.

The city was blanketed in a typical March fog. I like walking in the fog, like the feeling of isolation, of mystery. It was beginning to blow away by the time I reached the Embarcadero and I took a few minutes to stroll by the fleet of fishing boats, breathing in the tangy air. I love the smell of the sea, which may be why I've never gotten around to moving my office away from downtown Seattle.

I still arrived first and hovered near the cash register. I don't know how I was expecting Elliot Brill to look, but certainly not like he'd stepped out of a forties advertisement in Yachting magazine. He was just under six feet and his blond hair and blue eyes were set off by a fantastic tan. He was wearing a navy blue blazer with brass buttons, an ascot and had a yachting cap tucked under his arm. I'd never seen anyone dressed like that except in old drawing room comedies, the ones they show on late night TV.

His glance settled on me and he smiled. Shades of Cary Grant! His voice even had that same clipped accent. "You must be Miss Roarke. A pleasure to meet you. I'm Elliot Brill."

Before I could answer, a waitress fluttered up. "Mr. Brill. Your table is ready."

Taking my elbow he steered me after the waitress who conducted us to a corner table. I'm not much on being led around but his manners were so beautiful it seemed crass to object. I even let him hold my chair for me.

Floor to ceiling windows on two sides gave a magnificent view of the bay and the Golden Gate bridge. It was the kind of table to die for but Elliot Brill didn't even seem to notice, as if he'd sat at this table and viewed this view so often he didn't see it anymore.

I studied the menu with interest because my stomach was already rumbling. Brill ordered fresh squeezed orange juice, tea and a toasted muffin. I wasn't having any of that. I wanted food. He stared at me with a stunned look, like maybe I had two heads or something, as I settled for a pecan waffle with an order of crisp bacon and eggs over easy on the side, juice and coffee. I suppose he was used to women who dined on toast points and weak tea.

People like Elliot Brill, old money people, tend to intimidate me, particularly in social situations. I was raised strictly middle class, and despite Tony's trust fund, I'm still middle class in a lot of ways. I'll probably never be anything else, at least socially.

He related a couple of amusing San Francisco anecdotes while we waited for the food, then kept up the light chatter while we ate. Apparently, in his world, one didn't discuss serious topics during a meal. That was okay with me. I like to concentrate on my food. Finally the waitress took away our empty plates and refilled our cups.

I sat back and smiled. "Ready for business?"

He cocked a quizzical eyebrow and the corners of his mouth lifted slightly. "Do we have business?"

"Have the Seattle police been in touch with you?"

His left eyebrow shot higher. "No, they haven't. Is there some reason why they should?"

"I understand Arthur Trent stayed with you a couple of weeks ago. Are you old friends?"

There was a wariness in his blue eyes that surprised me. "I suppose we were at one time. We were in college together but that was twenty years ago."

"But you've kept in touch, stayed friends, haven't you?"

The wariness became more pronounced. "Not really. Just the annual Christmas card sort of things. I hadn't seen Art in years until a couple of weeks ago?"

I was surprised and I suppose it showed. I hadn't made that many friends in college, but those I had are important to me and I make a practice of keeping in touch.

"Other than our studies, we didn't have that much in

common." His tone was defensive. "Once we graduated, we went our separate ways. I'm surprised Art sent you to see me. Our reunion wasn't exactly a success. What's this all about?"

"Arthur Trent's wife has disappeared."

I wasn't prepared for his reaction. His face blanched, turning a sickly yellow under his tan, and for a moment I thought he might faint. His teacup rattled as he placed it in the saucer. His shock seemed a little excessive. I leaned forward, suddenly suspicious. "I understand Arthur Trent spent the weekend of March eighteenth through the twenty-first with you."

He nodded and made a visible effort to pull himself together, but I could tell his mind was elsewhere. "Was that when she disappeared?" he asked.

"She was last seen on the morning of the nineteenth. Did you meet Arthur's plane?"

"No. We didn't actually get together until Friday afternoon."

"He didn't stay with you Thursday night?"

"He stayed at my place. At least, I assume he did. I was delivering a boat to a customer in Los Angeles and didn't get back until late morning on Friday. Art had already left for the luncheon in Berkeley. I only got there for the tail end of it."

His voice was back to normal but there was still a haunted look in his eyes and his hand trembled as he sipped his tea. I was trying to think of a way to question his reaction, when he asked, "When you say his wife disappeared, do you mean that she left him or that she... she literally disappeared?"

I thought the question odd. Hadn't he been listening when I'd asked if the Seattle police had contacted him? There was something here I didn't understand. "She dropped off some cleaning on Friday morning. That's the last time she was seen as far as we have been able to determine."

He stared out over the bay, and his body trembled. "God, it's like a nightmare occurring all over again." I waited but he said nothing more.

"Again?" I prompted.

"Marie, my wife. The same thing happened." His voice was flat, dead. "It was a Sunday morning. We'd been out late the night before. I was still half asleep when she left. I remember her saying she was going to run down to Alouette." I raised an eyebrow. "The bakery. They make marvelous croissants. It was almost a ritual. Marie went out for croissants or brioches and the paper every Sunday morning. This time she never came back. I never saw her again."

I felt like someone had punched me in the gut. Coincidence. It had to be.

He stood up suddenly. "I can't talk about this now. Where are you staying?"

I told him and watched him pull a handful of bills out of his pocket and drop them on the table without counting them. "I'll call you later."

He walked out of the restaurant like a blind man stumbling through a maze. I had to stop to collect my coat and by the time I got outside, Elliot Brill had disappeared. I stood on the sidewalk wondering what to do next. The cold that chilled my bones wasn't entirely due to the wind off the bay.

I walked toward the cable car stop. There were a lot more questions I wanted to ask Brill, but as shaken as he was, I knew he wouldn't be calling for some time, if at all. I didn't want to sit around my hotel room waiting and couldn't think of anything else to do until I talked with Brill again.

I got off the cable car in China Town. If I had to kill time, I might as well kill it doing something I enjoyed. I wandered down the street, window-shopping. An ivory carving of a bridge caught my eye and I stopped to admire the delicate workmanship.

The eight tiny figures on the bridge were carved in incredible detail. I was particularly intrigued by an old man, bent nearly double under a load of fire wood, each branch of wood with its distinctive knots and burls. The sculptor had captured a look of infinite weariness and patience on the old man's face. Behind the old man, a young girl danced across the bridge, her face and figure radiating joy. I had to have the carving!

I'd only been vaguely aware of two elderly Chinese, leaning against the wall next to the door, discussing the younger generation's lack of respect for their elders. It wasn't until I entered the shop that I realized they were speaking in Chinese and that I'd understood a good deal of the conversation. The subliminal language lessons were working.

I was feeling the heady rush of accomplishment as I approached the old woman behind the counter. I was feeling so good, in fact, that I didn't hesitate when I wrote the check in five figures for the carving.

I spent the rest of the morning wandering up and down the street eavesdropping on conversations and buying a lovely silk cheongsam for myself and another for Mary Sue and a couple of gifts for Carmen and my mother.

Back at the hotel, I carried my loot up to my room. There was no blinking light on the phone so I knew Elliot Brill hadn't called. I'd walked up an appetite and decided to give him until after lunch. If he hadn't called by then, I'd try to reach him. I settled for soup and a sandwich from room service. While I waited for my food to arrive, I added my notes on our conversation to the file.

My lunch came and I ate. Still the phone didn't ring. I finally called but got his answering machine. I began to pace impatiently. I looked up his address and had almost decided to camp outside his door when the phone rang.

I snatched up the receiver. "Roarke."

Elliot Brill immediately began to apologize for leaving me at the restaurant.

I cut him off. "Mr. Brill, I really need to see you. There are a number of questions I need answered."

"Who exactly are you, Miss Roarke? When you called this morning, I assumed you were a friend of Art's, but this isn't a social visit, is it?"

"No, it isn't. I'm a private investigator hired originally to find Maureen Trent."

"Did Art hire you?"

"I can't give the name of my client, Mr. Brill. I can only tell you that my job has expanded to include learning more about Arthur, clearing him, if possible."

"Clearing him of what?"

"He left a message on his computer saying he couldn't take any more. The police are taking his message as a confession that he killed his wife."

There was silence on the other end of the line, then he said, "And you're here to establish an alibi?"

"No, Mr. Brill, I'm here to try to learn the truth. If Arthur Trent didn't kill his wife, someone else did. Until it's established that Mr. Trent couldn't have done it, the police aren't going to look much farther."

He didn't answer, so I continued. "Look, I really need some background, somewhere else to look."

"Why are you asking me? Can't Art tell you what you want to know?"

"Mr. Brill, your friend tried to commit suicide. He's currently in a coma."

There was another heavy silence on the line, then a sigh and he asked, "What do you want to know?"

"Well, for starters, how long have you known Arthur"

"We met at Berkeley. We were both studying naval architecture. There were four of us that hung around together all through college. Art, Seth, Dale, and myself. We were all interested in designing pleasure boats. We called ourselves the Four Boatniks."

"The what?"

"I know it sounds stupid but we were really just a bunch of kids then. Instead of Musketeers, we used Boatniks.

"Sounds like you were very close."

"I suppose we were, but that was a long time ago. We... we drifted apart. After all, we were involved in our own careers, that sort of thing." He sounded a little too defensive.

"I understood he was in San Francisco for some kind of reunion."

"No. No. There was a symposium at the University. Art and Seth were here for that."

"Seth?"

"Seth Steiner. You should probably talk to him. He flew in on Wednesday. He'd know when Art arrived. He and Art were probably together before I got back. He was always closer to Art than I was. There isn't much more I can tell you."

"Just a couple more questions. If you hadn't seen each other in twenty years, why was Arthur Trent staying with you?"

"Seth was chairing the symposium. We were all attending. I...with the hotel situation what it is... when Seth called, well, I couldn't turn them down."

"When did Mr. Steiner contact you?"

"Dr. Steiner. A couple of months before. Look, I really can't help you. I don't know anything about Art's private life, didn't even know he had married. I don't want to get involved."

He gave me Seth Steiner's address and phone number in Boston before he hung up.

I added this conversation to my notes, then sat at the table reading and re-reading them. None of it made sense yet. But one thing I was sure of: Elliott Brill had not been happy to see his old college buddies. I wondered why.

I checked my watch. Two-thirty in San Francisco was five-thirty in Boston. I took a chance and called the office number Brill had given me. It turned out to be the Massachusetts Institute of Technology. I was informed that Dr. Steiner was not on campus. I tried his home number but there was no answer.

I called Ian Donlevy and learned Trent was still in a coma and Maureen was still missing. I told him he would be receiving a typed report of my Seattle investigation and then repeated what Elliot Brill had told me. "I think I should go to Boston and interview Dr. Steiner in person. If he can verify that Arthur Trent was in San Francisco, I'll get a notarized affidavit. That should at least get the police to widen their investigation."

"Go ahead. Do whatever you feel is necessary." He sounded depressed.

"Has something else happened that I should know about?"

"The police have been going through Arthur's things. They found a marriage certificate. Apparently he married a Belinda Montgomery in Yuma, Arizona in 1979. They didn't find any divorce papers."

CHAPTER SIX

I called American Airlines and reserved a seat on their red-eye flight. They also confirmed a room for me at the Lenox Hotel in Boston, guaranteeing it with my American Express card. The concierge found me a box, tape, packing material and shipping labels for the results of my shopping spree. When I had it packed, he arranged for UPS to pick it up.

I called Carmen and told her I'd be away longer than expected and not to look for me until she saw me. I also told her to expect the package but not to open it.

Knowing I wouldn't get any sleep on the flight, I decided it was worth paying another night's tariff to take a long nap. After showering, I crawled in bed but sleep wouldn't come. Instead, my mind churned like a washing machine on the heavy cycle.

From everything I'd learned about Maureen Donlevy Trent, she wasn't a nice person. A lot of people seemed to have a reason to dislike, even hate, her. Enough to commit murder? Hell, murders were committed for a lot more stupid reasons. It happened every day.

For that matter, she might not even be dead. Had she run off with another man? Possibly, but from everything I'd learned about her, I doubted it. She hadn't cleaned out their bank account. At least I assumed she hadn't or Ian would have said something. I'd have to remember to ask him. She hadn't taken any of her clothes, either, unless she'd removed them from the house earlier. When I got back to Seattle, I wanted to take a look inside the Trent house.

Had Maureen been kidnapped? Doubtful. There'd been no ransom demands. Kidnappers didn't usually wait two weeks to contact the family with their demands.

I remembered reading, as a teenager, a paperback romance where a lovesick European aristocrat had held an American girl captive and forced her to marry him. I thought it a perfectly ridiculous plot at the time. It seemed even more ridiculous now. I couldn't imagine anyone that fascinated with Maureen, unless maybe Mark Kiner. Of course there was the guy back east that had imprisoned the little girl, but Maureen was no child. There are a lot of weirdos out there, but I still couldn't picture Maureen inciting that kind of obsession.

I mentally listed the people I'd met who might hold a grudge against her. At the top of the list was Arthur. *If* he knew she was playing around. That was a big if. Mark Kiner. *If* he had been out of the hospital at the time. Myron Westover. He obviously hated Maureen for what she'd done to Mark. But did he hate her enough? Connie Phillips? Had she finally figured out that Maureen had been using her all these years?

I gave up trying to sleep. Taking a yellow pad from by briefcase, I started a list of things to check when I returned to Seattle. Like where had each person been when Maureen disappeared. I still wanted to interview Anson Penman and Claudia Oliver. I hadn't checked out Tree Alert yet, either. And where in the hell was her car?

I tossed the pad back in my briefcase and got dressed. It only took me a few minutes to finish my packing. I carried my bag downstairs, checked out, and rode the hotel van to the airport.

The flight was just as miserable as I expected it to be. I'm not that fond of flying in the first place and I was crammed in the center of a three-seat row. In the window seat, an elderly lady with denture breath was soon snoring louder that Snoqualmie Falls at full flood. On my left was a punk rocker who obviously didn't believe in bathing and twitched and jerked like a junkie going through withdrawal.

Of course, he could have been responding to music; he had a pair of earphones clamped over his head. If he was, I was glad I couldn't hear it. Punk rock is not my style. But then I've been told I have weird taste in music. I prefer classical or country and I even like elevator music.

During the flight, I tried to concentrate on the case, but for some reason, memories of my father kept crowding in. Pop had been a red-headed, laughing Irishman, always singing Irish folksongs in a rich tenor or cracking jokes. He'd come to America at the age of twelve, to live with an uncle in Boston. He'd quit high school and gone to sea on a merchant ship when Great Uncle Sean had died. Dad had worked his way up to Master Seaman and saved his pay, intending to return to Ireland when he had enough to buy a pub.

Those plans had changed upon meeting my mother when his ship had called in Seattle. He'd wandered into an art gallery to get out of the rain. Mom and several other art students had been studying the exhibit.

At that point in the story, Pop would always turn and wink at Mom before saying, "She was the prettiest picture in the place. A Madonna. I lost me heart the minute I laid eyes on her. I followed her home, then hied meself back to the ship, collected me gear, jumped ship and niver looked back. Not that the citadel was easily breached, lassie. Nay, it took me nearly four years to convince my lady to have me. But it was worth the wait. Remember that, lassie: anything worth having is worth waiting for."

The memories brought a lump to my throat and an emptiness in my heart. After all these years, I still missed my father terribly. I greeted the "fasten seat belts" announcement with relief.

Boston was in the grip of a late cold snap. The temperature was hovering just below freezing and the air smelled like snow. I'd never been to Boston, and despite my tiredness, craned my neck to take in the sights, not that I saw much on the short ride. It was still too dark.

I was so tired my bones ached as I followed the bellman to my room. I waited impatiently for him to make the little adjustments to the heat and other things they feel they have to do to earn a bigger tip. When he was finally gone, I stripped, threw on my nightgown and whipped back the covers. Real pillows! Real, honest-to-god, human size pillows.

My mental alarm clock went off two hours later but short-circuited before I was more than half awake. When I finally awoke, it was nine o'clock, but at least I was refreshed and eager to get on with the investigation.

I debated calling for an appointment with Dr. Steiner, then decided against it. I might learn more if I took him by surprise. Assuming, of course, that Elliot Brill hadn't warned him.

I stopped at the desk to let them know my stay would be indefinite, got directions to the MIT campus and headed for the hotel dining room and a big breakfast. It was spitting snow when I stepped outside and much too cold for my light raincoat. I grabbed a taxi and had him drop me off at the administration building. It was an old brick building with wide concrete steps. I trudged up and into the huge lobby.

It took a while to find someone who even knew of Dr. Steiner and to get directions to the proper building. And, of course, I got lost. I was shivering so hard by the time I finally entered the right building, I was afraid my muscles would never unwind and I'd go through the rest of life permanently hunched. I still hadn't thawed by the time I found Steiner's office.

I can't believe how much younger college kids are these days. The girl who was typing in the tiny front office looked about sixteen. Maybe she was one of those whiz kids, but if so, her smarts didn't include intelligent conversation. When I asked to speak to Dr. Steiner, she just stared at me.

"This is his office, isn't it?" I asked.

She hesitated, then nodded.

"Is he in?"

She shook her head. Was she a mute? I'd always heard MIT attracted the best brains in the country, I hoped she wasn't a sample. I tried again. "When do you expect him?"

"Who?"

Well, at least she could speak, perhaps she was retarded. I repeated slowly, enunciating clearly, "I wish to speak to Dr. Seth Steiner. What time do you expect him?"

"Oh. He's not on campus."

I was making progress. She'd spoken a complete sentence. "Where is he?"

She pursed her mouth and frowned. "In London."

My heart sank. "When do you expect him back?"

"I don't."

I resisted the urge to tear at my hair, or better yet, at hers. "Do you mean he's no longer—"

"I mean, it's not my place to expect him."

My glance sharpened. There was actually a twinkle in those pale blue eyes. The kid had a sense of humor. Unfortunately I was in no mood to appreciate it. "Look, I've just flown in from San Francisco. It is imperative I speak to Dr. Steiner as soon as possible. If you know when he is returning, I'd like to know. I really don't want to have to fly to London."

"Dr. Steiner is participating in a series of lectures in London that last through Friday, uh, tomorrow. He has a ten o'clock class on Monday so I suppose he'll be back Saturday night or Sunday. That's all I know."

I stomped out in a thoroughly bad mood. The fact that it was snowing harder and there were no taxis cruising the campus did nothing to lighten my mood. By the time I'd walked back to the administration building, my pumps were soaked and my feet felt like slabs of frozen beef. I found a phone, called a taxi, and went back to the hotel. If taxi rates are high in Seattle, in Boston they are astronomical. It would be cheaper to rent a car.

I filled the tub with hot water and eased myself into it, watching my skin change from blue to red, letting the heat melt the chill out of my body and brain. I don't usually let little things get under my skin, but this whole case was beginning to make me antsy.

There might not be a body but I was convinced that Maureen Trent was dead. I don't like murder. The fact that I had talked or might be going to talk to a murderer gave me the willies. I wasn't exactly scared but I wasn't comfortable, either. Murder can be habit forming.

Thoroughly depressed, I climbed out, toweled myself off and padded barefoot into the bedroom and wrapped myself in my robe. I lit a cigarette, picked up the phone, and called my client.

Ian sounded as depressed as I felt. There had been no change in Arthur Trent's condition and the doctor's weren't hopeful. The police were still convinced Arthur had killed Maureen but didn't seem to be making much progress.

"Who's handling the case," I asked.

"Detective McCready."

That surprised me. Why hadn't Sam told me? I pushed the question away. "Dr. Steiner is in London. He's not expected back until Saturday or Sunday. Do you want me to wait for him?"

He sighed and told me to stick around, that he'd pay for my time and expenses.

After I hung up, I paced the floor awhile, then dressed. It was my last clean outfit. I called down and informed the desk that I'd be staying until Monday, arranged to have my clothes cleaned and back the next day, and for a rental car to be delivered to the hotel. I looked up Seth Steiner in the phone book and copied down his address. I might as well check the guy out.

I didn't relish spending the weekend in a strange city, not this time of year. If the weather had been decent, I'd have enjoyed the time to explore. So much early American history had taken place within a few miles. But tramping through the cold and snow didn't appeal to me.

My mood was deteriorating rapidly as I crammed my feet back into my wet shoes. I decided to indulge in that female panacea for all ills, shopping. The first thing I wanted was some warm footwear and a warmer coat.

Boyleston Street is a Mecca of small shops but the first thing that caught my eyes was a travel agency. A sign in the window advertised one-day skiing trips to Vermont. There were seats available on the charter bus trip on Saturday, the price was reasonable, and what the hell, there wasn't much I could do on the weekend, anyway. I wrote a check, collected my tickets, and was told the bus would pick me up at my hotel at six on Saturday morning.

I found a sportswear shop and splurged on a new two-piece ski suit, justifying the purchase by reminding myself that my old one was getting rather worn. Then I got carried away and bought a beautiful pair of Alaskan fur mukluks, some après ski boots, and heavy socks. In another shop I found wool slacks imported from England, a Norwegian sweater, and an English wool pantsuit. I began to enjoy myself. In a delightful little boutique I threw caution to the wind and bought masses of handmade lingerie from New Orleans and a silk blouse to go with my new suit. Of course, by then I had to buy something to pack them in, but my native caution took over and I settled for a cheap nylon sports bag.

By the time I got back to the hotel, my car was there. I completed the paper work, dashed upstairs, and changed into the mukluks and ski jacket, my mood considerably lightened.

The mukluks kept my toes toasty warm as I wormed my way through the horrendous traffic and across the Harvard Bridge into Cambridge. With the help of the free map that came with the car, I finally found the right street.

The address I'd copied from the phone book turned out to be a two-story frame house with bow windows, divided into two apartments. It was painted gray with white trim and the now heavily falling snow made it look like a typical New England Christmas card scene.

I found a parking space, crossed the street, and climbed the steps to the front porch. There were two doors; one in the center of the house, one to the far right. Number 35 was the one to the right. I pressed my face against the frosted glass window in the door, but all I could see was a flight of stairs. Twisting my neck, I saw a pile of mail scattered on the floor. I pushed the bell a couple of times, not expecting any response, then crossed the porch to Number 33 and rang the bell.

I was about to give up and leave, when the door opened the length of the security chain and querulous voice asked, "What do you want?"

"I'm sorry to bother you but I'm looking for Dr. Steiner."

"He's out of town."

I put on my most helpless, confused look and said, "Oh dear. I was so hoping to see him. I've come all the way from California."

The door closed and I heard the chain being released, then it opened wide to display an elderly lady wearing a gray wool dress that reached nearly to her ankles and matched the paint on the house. Her hair, pulled into a bun on the top of her head, was only a couple of shades lighter. She clutched two shawls around her bony shoulders with one hand. The one she extended towards me was thin and covered with liver spots. "Are you Abigail? Do come in, child, you'll freeze to death out there."

The skeletal fingers gripped my arm, tugging at the sleeve of my jacket. "Come. Come. Oh, my, Professor Steiner will be so pleased you've finally come. He always said you would come back. Really, dear child, you shouldn't have left him alone for so long. A wife's place is by her husband's side. It's time you came home."

CHAPTER SEVEN

She tugged me into hallway before I could respond and shut the door. "Ma'am, I'm–"

"Come along, dear. Why you must be half frozen. What you need is a nice hot cup of tea. Now don't argue. I've a pot all made."

She let go of my arm and led the way into the parlor. It was the only word to describe the room. If she looked like she'd just stepped out of a twenties movie, the room was purely Victorian. Two uncomfortable looking red velvet sofas faced each other in front of the fireplace, each with a round table shrouded with fringed cloths and cluttered with silver framed photos and porcelain figurines.

"Won't you be seated, my dear. I'll be right back with the tea," she said as she backed out of the room and disappeared down the hall.

I crossed to the fireplace to warm my hands. The one thing I'd forgotten during my shopping binge was gloves. The room was dim, the only light coming from the bow window and a standing lamp with a pink fringed shade. Wainscoting, dark with age, covered the lower half of the walls while Chinese wallpaper decorated the upper half. I couldn't resist moving closer to examine the paper. Running a finger over it I realized it wasn't paper but silk and from the feel, very old.

I moved back to the fire when I heard the rattle of silver and china. My hostess appeared a moment later wheeling an antique rosewood tea cart topped with a Georgian silver tea service that was obviously worth a small fortune. Cups and saucers and a plate of finger sandwiches nestled beside it. She pushed the cart between the sofas and seated herself.

"Do you take cream or lemon, Abigail?"

"My name is not Abigail," I said, moving to the opposite sofa and taking a seat. I took a card from my purse and handed it to her. "My name is Kerry Roarke. I'm a private investigator from Seattle."

She glanced at the card and then back to me. "I don't understand. I thought you said you were from California. You're not Abigail?"

"No, Ma'am. I came here from San Francisco to talk with Dr. Steiner."

"Oh, dear. The poor Professor will be so disappointed." She sighed and put my card aside. "Well, we'll still have our tea."

"Thank you, Mrs…"

"It's Miss. Miss Theodora Parkins. Now, do you take cream or lemon?"

"Neither, thank you."

She poured a cup and handed it to me, along with a dainty linen napkin. From the thinness of the fabric, I guessed the napkin was older than my hostess. The cup was so delicate I was almost afraid to pick it up but the tea was something special. I'd never tasted any quite like it and said so.

Her face lit up and she smiled. "It's a special blend from China. My family has received a tin of it every year for over a hundred and fifty years. My great-great-grandfather was one of the first China traders, you know.

"My, it's nice to have someone in to tea. Most of my friends have passed on. Young people now don't seem to have time to take tea."

She was relaxed; although at no point did her back touch the sofa. A pose I couldn't emulate even if I'd wanted to. I wondered how many hours she'd had to wear a backboard to acquire that perfect posture.

"Have you known Dr. Steiner long," I asked.

"Oh, yes. I knew his grandmother. His mother, too, before she married and moved to California. Such a lovely young woman. When Professor Steiner took up his position at the Institute, I was the first person he came to see. I'd never considered taking in boarders but he needed a place to stay. His grandmother's house had been sold after her death, you see. The remodeling was quite a trial on my nerves but it all worked well in the end."

"When do you expect Dr. Steiner to return?"

"He told me he would return on Sunday. Did Abigail send you?"

"Abigail?" I asked.

"His wife. Will she be returning soon?"

"I'm afraid I don't know. I've never met her. Is she visiting in California?"

"I really don't know. I assume she is still there, although now that you mention it, the Professor never said."

"When did she leave? Did she go to San Francisco with him earlier this month?"

For the first time, Miss Parkins appeared flustered. "Oh, no. She's didn't come to Cambridge with him. Hasn't even visited him in all these years."

"Are they divorced?"

"Dear me, no. Why the Professor absolutely adores her, misses her terribly. That's why I was so hoping you... well, she'll come home someday."

Her hands fluttered to the teapot. "Won't you have some more tea?"

"Thank you, but I must go. I'll stop by again on Sunday evening. Would you tell Dr. Steiner that it's very important I speak with him?"

"Of course, my dear."

She walked me to the door, invited me to drop by for tea any afternoon, and assured me she would give the Professor my card as soon as he returned.

I drove back to my hotel, only getting lost twice. I hate one-way streets. Leaving my car to be valet parked, I went to my room, more than ready to call it a day. A long, hot soak in the tub refreshed me and I dressed again. Opening my briefcase on the table, I pulled up a chair and added notes on my conversation with Miss Parkins, then re-read all of my previous notes.

I kept coming back to the fact that Maureen had left her husband, suddenly and without warning. Marie Brill had left her husband almost the same way. Could there be a connection?

I looked at my watch. Four-ten. In San Francisco it would be one-ten. I dug through my notes, found Elliot Brill's phone number and dialed. After the tenth ring, when I was about to give up, he answered.

"Mr. Brill, this is Kerry Roarke. I have one more question to ask. When did you're wife disappear?"

There was a long silence and I was beginning to wonder if he'd hung up on me, when he answered, "March 22, 1985."

"Oh." It was all I could think to say.

"May I ask why you want to know?"

"Just a wild idea. I hadn't realized it was that long ago. I'm sorry to bother you."

"No problem. Did you talk to Seth?"

"Not yet. He's at a seminar or something in London. I'm waiting for him to return. By the way, did you ever meet his wife?"

"No, I didn't."

"Do you know when they were married?"

"Not really. I think it was around 1984 or 85."

"You weren't invited to the wedding?"

"I don't remember. I might have been. Actually, I suppose I was."

"But you didn't go?"

"No."

I thanked him and hung up. There was something here I didn't understand. Four guys, great pals all through college, then boom–nothing. No personal contact in almost twenty years. No dropping in when they were in town, no phone calls, no sharing of triumphs and griefs. The press of business, separate lives? Bull shit! Something had happened.

I didn't like the road my thoughts were taking. It was simply too wild. And it was too soon to be making any guesses, wild or otherwise. I didn't have enough information. But I sure as hell wanted to talk to Dr. Steiner.

I packed away the file, ordered a sandwich from room service, and turned on the television, determined to put the case out of my mind. Television programming was no help. I had no interest in the local news.

I ate, then paced the room, feeling as caged as a tiger in a zoo. I paused at the window, staring down at the city, watching the street lights come on.

Boston. It was to this city, spread out before me, that my father had come to as a child. Suddenly I wanted to be out in the city, to try to see it as it must have appeared to him when he first arrived. Pulling on my mukluks and grabbing my coat, I left the hotel.

I wove my way through the crowds of exiting workers and walked the streets. Snippets of Pop's anecdotes came and went through my mind. A fight in McGonigle's Bar, lifting a pint in the Shamrock Pub, old Liam O'Shaunessey who hadn't known a sober day in his life but sang like an angel, Paddy O'Brien serenading Maggie Somebody and getting arrested for creating a public disturbance. I walked for hours, barely noticing the cold and the snow, feeling closer to my father than I had since his death. I finally wound up back at the hotel, cold and exhausted, but somehow comforted.

Friday was a gray day, the sky overcast but at least it wasn't snowing. After breakfast, I sat in the lobby trying to decide what to do next. At home, I'd have had little trouble checking out Dr. Steiner but Boston was a whole new ball game. Here I had no contacts, not even access to a computer. What I could do was get background information on the Steiner family, not that I thought any of it would pertain to locating Maureen Trent.

The Boatniks intrigued me. I sensed a mystery and I wanted to know more about them, simply to satisfy my own curiosity. It was a way to kill time, and who knows...

By four o'clock I'd learned that Seth Steiner was the son of Marcus Steiner and Isobel Whitman Steiner: that Isobel was the daughter of Bartholomew Whitman and Alice Toynbridge; that Isobel Whitman and Marcus Steiner had been married in 1952. I had also learned that Bartholomew Whitman had died in 1964 leaving an estate of over a million dollars to his wife, Alice, and a bequest of one hundred thousand dollars to his daughter, Isobel. At that time, Isobel had been living in Pasadena, California. Alice Toynbridge Whitman had died in 1978, leaving her estate to Seth Steiner of Pacific Palisades, California. The estate had grown to over two million dollars. In 1979, Seth Steiner had sold the Whitman house to a couple named Carstairs. Interesting but hardly applicable to the case of the missing sister.

I'd also visited the campus of MIT and talked to a couple of Dr. Steiner's students. I learned that Dr. Steiner was well liked if somewhat pedantic, was a hard taskmaster but a fair grader, and was considered brilliant. I also learned more about naval architecture than I ever wanted to know.

In the library I found copies of several articles authored by Dr. Steiner in learned journals, none of which I understood. I did find a picture of him in a group faculty photo. I studied the picture with interest. He appeared to be of average height, slender, with a long, ascetic face, a receding hairline, and sad eyes. I tried to photocopy the picture but it came out so blurred I threw it away.

Leaving MIT, I decided I might as well do a little sightseeing. I wanted to visit the Harvard campus but the traffic intimidated me. I'd thought traffic was bad in Seattle, but it was nothing compared to the Boston area. I gave up and drove back to the hotel.

In my room, I glanced through the "Things To Do" pamphlet and saw that the Boston Symphony would be performing that night. Shrugging into my coat again, I walked to Symphony Hall and purchased a ticket. On the walk back, I decided to have dinner after the concert. I made reservations at the Lenox Pub and Grill on my way upstairs. I transferred my notes on Dr. Steiner to the file, decided I was hungry, and ordered a sandwich from room service.

The concert was great, the dinner excellent, and I went to bed in a better frame of mind that I'd been since I reached

Boston.

I was downstairs the next morning a few minutes before six. I dozed during most of the bus trip to Vermont but was wide-awake and eager by the time I'd rented boots and skis and headed for the lifts. The sun was shining, the temperature just below freezing and the snowstorm had coated the slopes with fine powder. The skiing was absolutely perfect. When the bus dropped me back at the hotel, I was physically exhausted but mentally and emotionally recharged.

I slept late on Sunday, read the paper over a leisurely breakfast, and decided to spend the afternoon exploring Cambridge and the Harvard campus.

Even on Sunday, finding a parking place wasn't easy but I finally squeezed in between a Ford Bronco and ancient Austin-Healy Sprite. Harvard Square was not what I'd imagined it to be. Not really a square at all. I wandered leisurely, intrigued by the tiny cafes offering a multitude of exotic cuisine. I paused in front of the Coop to watch two bearded men, dressed in ragged jeans and dirty ponchos, their bare feet clad only in leather sandals, arguing violently over the poetry of William Blake. Even in my mukluks, my toes chilled at the sight and I wondered if theirs would be frostbitten by the time they got home.

In a music store I found the widest selection of recorder music I'd ever seen and a treasure trove of Elizabethan and baroque music. My purchases made my earlier shopping spree pale by comparison. I came away gleefully clutching my new treasures.

The recorder is not a popular instrument. I'd been introduced to it as a child by an old man who'd lived above my parent's liquor store. When he'd been taken away to a nursing home by his son, he'd given me his soprano recorder. I still have it but prefer my alto. I frequently play with a quartet made up of a flute, viol, and violin. We play mostly for our own enjoyment, although occasionally we perform in public, for fanciers of Elizabethan music.

I spent time in several bookstores, bought a book on Chinese porcelain and a couple of paperback novels, then spent more time in the language tape section. My subliminal Chinese lessons were obviously working; perhaps I'd try Russian next, or maybe Japanese or Arabic.

At Nini's, I turned the corner and wandered into Brattle Square then back to Harvard Square. It was all interesting but I think I prefer the Pike Place Market in Seattle. I stopped in one of the cafes for a cup of coffee. It was drinkable but definitely not Starbucks. Two couples at the table on my right were discussing existentialism so I tuned them out. The conversation on my left was much more interesting. They were speaking French and I was pleased I could understand every word of the discussion on the sexual practices of some tribe in New Guinea.

I finished my coffee, used the rest room, and walked back to my car. I'd called the airport before I left the hotel and gotten the arrival times of direct flights from London. The TWA flight would be arriving in a few minutes, the British Airways flight wouldn't arrive for another two hours. I wasn't taking any chances. I wanted to be at the house when Dr. Steiner arrived, before Miss Theodora Parkins had time to give him my card. I'd decided I wanted surprise on my side.

Not only did I want to know if Arthur Trent had indeed been in San Francisco at the time his wife had disappeared but I also wanted to know why a four-year college friendship had suddenly shattered.

CHAPTER EIGHT

I parked two doors away Steiner's house and killed the motor. Fifteen minutes and two cigarettes later, the cold drove me to start the motor and turn the heater back on. The house I'd parked in front of was also a two story wood frame, but not as well maintained as Miss Parkins' house. Shortly after I turned the car back on, the curtain in a downstairs window fluttered and I saw a white face peering out. A few minutes later, the face appeared again and I knew my waiting in the car wasn't going to work. The one thing I didn't need was some neighbor reporting a "suspicious person" to the police.

I was about to see if Miss Parkins had meant her tea invitation when a cab pulled up and a man I assumed was Dr. Steiner got out. He was wearing a heavy overcoat with a muffler wrapped around his neck and chin. Lugging an old leather suitcase, he mounted the steps, crossed to the side door, and pulled a key chain from his pocket. By the time he had the door open I was on the porch.

I glided across the porch and was in the door before he could close it. He was bending over, collecting the mail when he saw me. He gave a startled grunt and straightened up.

"Dr. Steiner? Dr. Seth Steiner?" I asked.

"Yes. Do I know you?" He peered at me myopically, then shook his head. "Who are you?"

"Kerry Roarke. I need to talk to you."

He edged away from me and picked up his suitcase.

"Well, call my office tomorrow."

"I need to talk with you now."

His glanced flicked to the mail in his hand and back to me. "I don't see students at home. You'll have to come to my office. I suggest you make an appointment."

I wanted to prick his pomposity. "I'm not one of your students. I'm a private investigator from Seattle. I really need to talk to you right away." I hesitated, then added, "I'm here on behalf of Arthur Trent."

In the dim light, I couldn't read his expression but I thought I saw his eyes widen "Artie? Artie sent you?"

"Actually, it was Elliot Brill who gave me your name and suggested I talk to you. Please, Doctor, may I come in? I won't take much of your time."

"Young lady, I've just returned from an exhausting trip. Can't this wait until tomorrow?"

"Time is of the essence, Doctor," I said, mimicking his precise accent.

"Oh, very well. Come along."

I followed him up the stairs and down a short, dark hall to the living room at the front of the house. He turned on the overhead light, tossed the mail on an antique cherry wood table, and motioned me in. "Have a seat, I'll be with you in a moment."

I slipped out of my jacket and tossed it on a ladder-back chair beside the table then looked around. It was definitely a man's room. All of the furnishing, except the table and chair by the door, were large, heavy, and obviously selected for comfort and utility. Two Morris chairs, covered in dull green wide-wale corduroy faced each other near the fireplace. Each had a heavy oak side table topped with a reading lamp. One chair and its matching ottoman was well worn, its table top

79

cluttered with a large ashtray, a pipe rack holding several pipes with well chewed ends and humidor.

I took the opposite chair. Over the oak mantel was a full-length portrait of a young woman, not beautiful but with a definite look of class and breeding. It was the kind of portrait you would expect to find in one of the stately homes of England, but not in a small apartment. I studied it, wondering if it was a painting of Abigail. If her haughty expression was anything to go by, I thought she and Steiner were made for each other.

Dr. Steiner returned, minus his overcoat and muffler.

He was wearing a tweed jacket with the obligatory leather patches on the sleeves, turtleneck sweater and pleated wool pants. Without looking at me, he walked across the room and opened an oak chest that turned out to be a liquor cabinet. Selecting a decanter and two snifters, he brought them across the room. Gently nudging the humidor out of the way, he set the glasses on the table and poured half an inch in one.

"I don't know about you, young lady, but I need something to get rid of the chill," He handed me the glass. I rarely drink and would have much preferred a cup of Miss Parkins' tea. Still, I wasn't about to offend him, at least not until I'd gotten the information I'd come for. I rolled the snifter between my palms as I'd seen done in the movies and waited while he poured himself a more generous amount and settled in the other chair.

Watching him, I decided he'd already had a few. With his bankroll, I pictured him flying first class and taking advantage of the free booze. Not that he was drunk, but he sure as hell wasn't cold sober either.

When he'd taken a couple of sips, he looked across at me with a slight smile. "You've come all of the way from the west coast?"

I nodded. "Elliot Brill said something about you being one of the Four Boatniks."

He smiled and some of the haughtiness disappeared. "It's been years since I've heard that. The Four Boatniks. Elliot Brill, Dale Lockman, Artie Trent, and myself. That does bring back memories."

"You were in college together? Is that when you met?"

His eyes closed and he chuckled, a deep, rasping sound. "The Four Boatniks. That does bring back memories. How young we were then."

"Have you stayed close friends all these years?"

His eyes flew open and the smile faded. "I couldn't say that. No, I couldn't say that."

"When was the last time you saw each other?"

"All together?" His brows drew together as he frowned. "Not since graduation."

"Individually, then."

"I haven't seen Dale in years. Get a card from him every Christmas. Last I heard he was in San Diego."

"The four of you were good friends all through college. Why did you split up so suddenly?"

His hand tightened on the snifter until I expected it to shatter and his lips thinned. A moment later he relaxed. "It was time to move on, my dear, to put away childish things and enter the rat race. It's called maturing."

"But–"

"What's done is done. Let the dead past bury its dead. Life is for the living. A pretty girl like you shouldn't be interested in the ramblings of an old man." He smiled again but I noticed the smile didn't reach his eyes. He added another inch of brandy to his glass and took a large swallow.

I was getting nowhere so I backed off. "You were closer to Arthur Trent?"

"True, I suppose. We were all close in college but then we went out separate ways. Elliot, of course, stepped into his father's business in San Francisco. Artie and I both worked at Consolidated Marine for a while after college."

He shot me a puzzled look. "You say you're here about Artie? What's he been up to?"

I decided to try for the information I needed first. "Did you see Arthur Trent when you were in San Francisco a couple of weeks ago?"

"Yes. He attended a symposium I chaired at the University of California, Berkeley."

"Did you see him Thursday night?"

He finished his brandy and poured another glass and took another sip. "Thursday. I think so."

"Are you sure? It's important."

"Well, let's see. I got in on Wednesday afternoon, went to Elliot's place to leave my luggage and freshen up. Took a cab over to the campus, met the other speakers and had dinner. That silly bugger, Bascomb, was there, so I left as soon as I could get away. But that was Wednesday and you want to know about Thursday. Hmmm. Let me think."

He drank again, leaned back, and closed his eyes. He took so long to continue, I was beginning to wonder if he'd dozed off. Finally he sat up, downed his drink, and poured another. "No, as a matter of fact, I didn't see Artie until Friday."

That wasn't what I wanted to hear. I asked, "Then he didn't arrive until Friday morning?"

There was a twinkle in his eye. "Oh, I suppose he came in Thursday night. We had a date for dinner Thursday night but..." His lips curved into a reminiscent, slightly drunken smile... "I ran into an old friend and was... detained."

"So you don't really know when Arthur Trent arrived?"

The smile vanished. "No. His things were there Friday morning when I came back to change. I assumed he had gone on to the campus in Berkeley. What's this all about?"

"What time did the symposium start?"

"One o'clock."

"Was he on time?"

"Yes. He was already seated in the front row when I took my place at the podium."

"Elliot Brill mentioned a luncheon. Did you attend? Did you see Mr. Trent?"

"Of course I was at the luncheon. I was seated at the head table. Artie could have been there, probably was, but I didn't see him. But then, I wasn't looking for him."

My mind was racing. Maureen had last been seen just before nine o'clock. Did that give Arthur Trent enough time to fly to San Francisco, leave his bag at Elliot Brill's place, and get across the bay? I'd have to check airline schedules.

"Miss...I've forgotten your name."

"Roarke. Kerry Roarke."

"Exactly who are you, Miss Roarke?"

"I'm a private investigator."

"Oh, yes. I believe you did mention that. And you are investigating Artie? What's he done? Can't be anything serious. Not old Artie."

He fumbled the top off the decanter, poured himself another shot, and put the bottle back without bothering to recap it. He was more stewed than I'd realized.

"Arthur Trent's wife disappeared Friday morning, March 19th. Trent attempted suicide a few days ago," I said, hoping my blunt words would sober him. They didn't.

Instead, his eyes filled with tears. "Poor old Artie. Well, I'm not surprised. He was terribly broken up when Buffy left him. Really went to pieces. Seemed to think he'd driven her away. Tried to tell him. Wasn't his fault. Just the way Buffy was."

"You knew his first wife?"

"Oh, yes. Cute little thing, all big blue eyes and the most magnificent blonde hair. Natural blonde. Belinda. Belinda Montgomery but everybody called her Buffy."

He leaned back again and closed his eyes. Tears streamed down his cheeks but he didn't seem to feel them. "Buffy. The nickname suited her, you know. She was wild about boats, always hanging around the marina. That's how we met her. Artie fell for her like the proverbial ton of bricks."

He took another drink without opening his eyes. "She loved the sun. As soon as we were out of the Marina, she'd go up on the foredeck, strip down, and sun bathe. That's how she got her nickname. Liked to sun bathe in the buff."

He sat up, gulped down the rest of the drink, and poured another. "Don't get me wrong. Buffy wasn't promish... promiscu–she wash...a nice girl. She jushed loved boats, loved the water, the sun. Loved life. Nice girl but shouldn't have married an old stick in the mud like Artie."

"She left him?"

He peered owlishly at me over the rim of his glass and nodded. "Just took off one day. There was a big yacht that sailed for Hawaii that day. Three young men. No matter what they say, I think she took off with them."

"Didn't Arthur try to find her?"

"Of course he did. Flew to Hawaii and spent a month trying to find her. Hounded the police and her parents, even hired a private detective."

"Her parents never heard from her?"

"No. Nobody did."

"Was she from California?"

"Oh, yes. El Monte."

"Are you sure her parents don't know where she is? Perhaps, she'd asked them not to tell Trent?"

"Nope. They liked Artie. If they'd heard, they'd have told him. She jushed disappeared."

"Not like Abigail." I don't know why I said it. The words just seemed to pop out of my mouth.

He sat up fast, his drink sloshing over his hand and staining his trousers. His eyes rolled wildly as he yelled. "No. No. Abigail didn't leave me. She'd never walk away without a word. She'll be back. Any day now. She'll be back."

"You and Trent stayed friends after you left college?"

"What? What?"

"You were obviously close after college. Why did the rest of you break up?"

He glared at me through unfocussed eyes. "Thash none of your bishness. Get out. Get out of here."

He lunged forward, lost his balance, and toppled sideways sending the humidor and brandy decanter flying. I scurried across the room and grabbed my coat. He lurched to his feet.
I dodged the brandy snifter he threw. It crashed into the wall. I dashed into the hall and down the stairs. I could hear him sobbing as I closed the front door.

I drove back to the hotel, my mind spinning. Buffy Trent had disappeared. Maureen Trent had disappeared. Marie Brill had disappeared. And, despite what Seth Steiner had said, my gut told me that Abigail Steiner had disappeared, too. Four women with nothing in common but the fact that their husbands knew each other.

And something had driven the four men apart. Had shattered a close friendship. Something neither Elliot Brill nor Seth Steiner was willing to talk about.

Two words pierced my mind like shards of glass, ripping, tearing. They reverberated through my mind in rhythm with the whop–whop–whop–of the tires.

Serial killer. Serial killer. Serial killer.

CHAPTER NINE

Serial killer. Like most Seattleites, the words sent a decided chill down my spine. We've had more than our share of serial killers. The atrocities of Ted Bundy and the Green River Killer are all too clear in our memories. No one can guess how many bodies are still hidden in our forested mountains. Almost monthly the grim remains of another victim are found. The words serial killer strike a special fear in many women in the Northwest and I'm not immune to that fear.

I had stopped quivering by the time I got back to the hotel and was beginning to get my thoughts under control. It was a wild idea and I tried to force it out of my mind. A serial killer didn't wait twenty years between killings. Well, it hadn't been twenty years but it had been a long time. Besides it was only supposition. I had no solid facts to go on.

I hurried to my room, called the airport, and got a seat on a late flight to Seattle. It took me only a few minutes to pack and check out of the hotel. I drove to Logan Airport, turned in my car, checked my two bags, and headed for the cafeteria. I wasn't hungry but acid was burning a hole in my stomach.

Airport food is as bad if not worse than airplane food. I ate a bowl of watery soup, corn muffins, and a glass of milk. My taste buds weren't satisfied but the pain stopped. I pulled out one of the books I'd purchased but couldn't get into it. I'd lost the ability to concentrate. It was a relief when they called my flight. I wanted to get home, to hug the dogs, lie in the

Jacuzzi until my body and mind unwound and then crawl into my own bed and sleep for twelve hours.

And that's exactly what I did. Almost.

The smell of coffee woke me and I glanced at the clock. Eight-thirty. I snuggled back down in bed, pulling the comforter up around my ears and closed my eyes but the scent was too enticing. Reluctantly I got up; six hours would have to do. With equal reluctance I did thirty minutes on the Nautilus and twenty minutes on the Nordic Track.

Slipping into an old pair of slacks and a sweatshirt, I went out to the stable, the dogs cavorting at my heels. I really didn't feel like riding but the mare I hoped to enter in a show needed work. I spent an hour in the ring taking her through her paces then headed back to the house feeling much more myself.

By the time I'd showered, dressed, petted the cat, and gone downstairs, Carmen had breakfast waiting. The exercise had given me an appetite that a stack of her blueberry pancakes made with fresh blueberries and served with home made blueberry syrup more than satisfied.

Carrying a mug of coffee, I started for the den, but the package in the front hall stopped me. Eagerly, I slit open the box, removed the gifts, and set them aside. I'd wrap them later and put them where Carmen would find them. Emotional thank yous always embarrass me, and both Carmen and my mother are emotional people. Carmen would thank me later in the way I liked best; a filet of beef Wellington or something equally special. After seven years she knew all my favorite foods.

Finally, I unwrapped the ivory bridge, caressing it gently with a fingertip, examining it closely for any shipping damage, but there was none. I carried it into the den and put it away in my safe. When I had the time, I'd call a friend who builds custom cabinets and have him make a special display case for it.

I would have liked to have spent the rest of the morning just looking at my treasure but duty before pleasure.

I'd been on the Maureen Trent case for a week and was no closer to locating her than when Ian Donlevy had first walked into my office. I got out the file and added notes on my conversation with Dr. Steiner. I collected all my receipts and entered them in my expense ledger, then scribbled out a complete report to date for Mary Sue to type. I added a note for her to send a copy to the client, called and left a message on her machine to pick it up.

That done, I decided what I needed was a long walk to try to get my thoughts in order. I called the dogs and started up one of the paths that headed towards Garfield Mountain, not that I planned to hike that far. The clouds were heavy and gray, crowding low against the mountains. The wet leaves shimmered silver in the dimness. Three hundred feet from the house, civilization disappeared and we were in a silent, primal world pungent with mingled scents of wet earth, decomposing vegetation and pine resin. I'd climbed this path so many times my feet took over leaving my mind free to wander.

Buffy Trent had disappeared sometime around 1980 or 81. Marie Brill had disappeared in 1985, or so Elliot Brill had said. I didn't know when Abigail Steiner had disappeared, if she had, but it had to be before 1987 when Dr. Steiner had moved to Boston, if Miss Parkins was to be believed. I couldn't think of any reason why she would lie.

Four women had disappeared. By choice or by force? They had disappeared over a period of at least twelve years. How could there possibly be any connection? Coincidence? Possibly.

I don't like coincidences.

But had they all actually disappeared? Dr. Steiner believed that Buffy had simply moved on to greener pastures. Perhaps she was a modern day Sadie Thompson, an aging beach bunny soaking up the sun in Tahiti or some other Pacific Island. It made as much sense as anything else.

What did I really know about Marie Brill? Only what her husband had told me. She went out for brioches and never came back. Had she had a lover waiting? Was she buried in some unknown grave, an unidentified victim of an overenthusiastic mugger?

As for Abigail Steiner, how did I know she was really missing? Dr. Steiner expected her to return at any time. After twelve years? I didn't know any of the circumstances. Perhaps she'd simply grown homesick and hopped a plane back to home, wherever that might be. Perhaps she hadn't wanted to give up the warmth of Southern California for the cold of Boston and was happily living her own life in the Los Angeles area.

What did it all add up to? Three wives had left their husbands. No big deal nowadays when half of all marriages ended in divorce. There couldn't possibly be any connection between the other women and the disappearance of Maureen Trent. Except, possibly Buffy. Had Arthur Trent wanted out of his first marriage? Not according to Dr. Steiner, but that didn't necessarily mean anything. Perhaps Buffy had been messing around and Arthur had killed her. With Maureen, had he seen history repeating itself? Maureen had disappeared from Seattle three weeks ago. It was the here and now I needed to concentrate on, not the past.

Shybaby came racing down the path, her excited barking snapping me out of my thoughts. White mist shrouded every thing beyond a couple feet and I realized I'd climbed farther than I'd planned. I was into the cloudbank. I whistled for Wiley, and when he appeared a moment later, we started back down. It was time to get to work.

After I showered again and changed into a navy blue pants suit with a canary yellow turtleneck and black ankle boots, I called Anson Penman's office and made an appointment to see him at four o'clock. I wanted to visit the Fiedler-McLaren offices, too. Why had Maureen walked out on a position she had worked years to achieve?

Driving into Seattle, I listened to a Clint Black tape, tapping my fingers on the wheel in time to the music, trying to put the case completely out of my mind and relax. I'd switched to a tape of chamber music by the time I located the mortgage company.

The girl at the front desk was new and hadn't known Maureen. She referred me to the Personnel Department. Fiedler-McLaren was no small outfit; they occupied four floors of the building. Personnel was at the back of the building on the third floor. Audrey Wickes was not cooperative, informing me only that Mrs. Trent had voluntarily left the company and that personnel records were privileged documents. Her attitude told me enough. Maureen Trent definitely wouldn't be welcomed back into the company fold.

I got off the elevator on the second floor and wandered down the hall, glancing into various offices, until a cute young thing in a miniskirt and boots asked me who I was looking for.

"Appraisals"

"Oh, they're on the fourth floor."

She escorted me back to the elevator, waited until it came, reached in and pushed the button and waved cheerily as the door closed.

I located the Appraisal Department, pushed open the door, and found myself face to face with a clone of my second grade teacher. She had the same corseted figure and her gray hair was pulled back into the same kind of knot at the nape of her neck. I resisted the urge to hang my head and clutch my hands behind my back as she glared down her nose at me.

"Yes?" Even her voice sounded like Mrs. Zachmeyer's.

"I'd like to speak to someone who knew Maureen Donlevy Trent."

Her glance raked me up and down. "Why?"

Hastily I dug out a card and handed it to her. "She's missing."

She hesitated a moment, tapping the card against her thumb. "Very well. Come this way."

I followed her down a short hall and through a door marked with the name Bruce Wilcox. The office was empty. She motioned me to a chair, closed the door, and took the seat behind the desk. "Mr. Wilcox is on vacation. We won't be disturbed. Now, what do you mean Mrs. Trent is missing?"

She sat, very upright, hands neatly folded on the desk while I explained. When I finished, she asked, "Why do you think her disappearance might have something to do with this company?"

"I don't. I'm looking for someone who can tell me something about her. She worked here for a number of years, she must have made some friends."

"She didn't. Maureen Trent was selfish, greedy, dishonest and completely without principle. She didn't make friends, she used people."

"Why did she quit?"

"She didn't. She was forced to resign to avoid prosecution."

Somehow that didn't surprise me, but I quirked an eyebrow and gave her a skeptical look. It worked.

"Mrs. Trent took kick-backs from sellers and real estate agents for appraising property beyond its market value. Among other things. She had no friends here, no one who knew her outside the office. You're wasting your time."

"I see. Well, thank you, Mrs.... ."

"Beidemeier."

Not Zachmeyer, but close.

I left Fiedler-McLaren and drove to Anson Penman's office on Martin Luther King Way in the Rainier Valley and found a parking spot right in front of his building.

I tossed an old sweater I keep in the car for that purpose over my briefcase. In this area, my Lincoln Town Car or any luxury car could easily be taken for that of a drug dealer and I didn't want some hophead thinking my briefcase was full of cocaine. After checking that all four doors were locked, and silently thanking Ford for the alarm system, I climbed the stairs between a pawn shop and a liquor store.

Penman's office was at the back of the building but the hall was well lit and had recently been painted a pale gray. I wondered how long it would be before the graffiti artists redecorated it. It was straight up four o'clock when I opened the door.

The woman behind the desk was young and could have given Whitney Houston a run for her money in the beauty department. The look she gave me wasn't beautiful and definitely not friendly. She made a production of checking her appointment calendar before asking, "You're K. K. Roarke?"

I gave her my best smile. "That's right. Is Mr. Penman in?"

"Can you tell me what this is regarding?"

I kept the smile firmly in place as I answered, "I'd prefer not to."

Her expression became even colder. I wondered how many clients had been driven away by her attitude. From the looks of the office, I didn't think Penman could afford to lose too many. Before she could respond, the door flew open.

Anson Penman looked like he might have played linebacker for the Seattle Seahawks. He was a big man, well over six feet, with wide shoulders and narrow hips. His skin was the color of milk chocolate and his hair, clipped short, was beginning to recede. He'd have been a handsome man if he'd shaved off the pencil-thin mustache.

He crossed the room in two strides, gave me a curious glance, then ignored me. "Bring me the Miller file and hold all my calls."

"This is Miss Roarke. She has a four o'clock appointment."

He turned back to me, his frown giving way to a forced smile. "Hello. I'm Anson Penman. Come on in." If this was the way all clients were greeted, I wondered how he managed to pay the rent. Maybe it was a race thing.

I followed him through a door on the left and took the chair he indicated. He settled into his chair, propped his elbows on the desk and leaned forward, resting his chin on tented fingers. "What can I do for you, Miss Roarke?"

I got right to the point. "When did you last see Maureen Trent?"

I can't say he paled, but his face turned a chalky brown, like a melted and cooled Hershey bar. His fingers clenched as he raised his head. "I beg your pardon?"

"Maureen Trent. I understand you worked together at Clean Sweep."

Some of the tension went out of his shoulders and his hands relaxed. "Maureen Trent." He repeated the name slowly as if trying to associate it with a face. "Oh, yes. I believe I do remember her. She gave us quite a large donation."

"I understand you introduced her to Clean Sweep."

He leaned back in his chair. "Now whatever gave you that idea?"

"Not what, who. Angela Bottoms said you introduced her into the group."

"Really? I'm afraid Angela has me mixed up with someone else. If I met Mrs. Trent prior to her involvement with Clean Sweep, I don't recall it."

"When was the last time you saw Mrs. Trent?"

He leaned forward again. "Would you mind telling me what this is about, Miss Roarke?"

"Not at all. Maureen Trent disappeared on the nineteenth of last month. We are trying to trace her movements. When did you see her last?"

"Are you with the police?"

"No." I pulled out one of my cards and slid it across the desk. "I'm a private investigator. I've been hired to locate her."

He glanced at my card, flicked it with a fingernail, and laid it aside. "You realize I don't have to answer any of your questions."

"Is there some reason for not answering them?"

"No. No, of course not. When did I last see Mrs. Trent?" He riffled through his desk calendar, then looked up. "I saw her on the sixteenth of March. We both attended a Clean Sweep meeting."

"You haven't seen her since?"

"No."

"Are you involved with Tree Alert?"

"No. I'm more interested in saving people than trees. Why do you ask?"

"I thought perhaps you might have met Mrs. Trent at one of their meetings." I changed the subject. "What was Mrs. Trent like the last time you saw her?"

"Like?" He shrugged, "Like always. What do you mean?"

"Did she seem nervous, excited, angry?"

I could almost see the wheels turning in his head and decided he probably wasn't a very good trial attorney.

"Well, I suppose she was a little angry."

"What about?"

He shrugged again. "She didn't think we were taking the right approach to the problems of the homeless. She thought we should be more... visible."

"More militant?"

"Exactly. She wanted to organize a protest parade, then picket City Hall." His smile was amused and faintly contemptuous. "Can you imagine how much success we'd have organizing the homeless into some semblance of order? Or getting them to march the distance she wanted? It simply wouldn't have worked. Besides, that's not the way we want to proceed."

"What about after the meeting?"

"I didn't see her after the meeting. In fact, if memory serves, I left a little early."

"And that was the last time you saw her?"

"That is correct."

"You have no idea where she might have gone?"

"None at all."

I stood up. "Thank you for your time. If I have any more questions, I'll call you."

He didn't bother to rise so I crossed the room and let myself out. As I opened the door into the outer office, his secretary was just sliding into the chair behind her desk.

Anson Penman was lying. About what, I wasn't sure, but something. People lie about the most ridiculous things. Lying doesn't necessarily make them guilty of anything more than bad judgment but it doesn't make my job any easier. I'd have to take a closer look at Anson Penman.

CHAPTER TEN

I drove north, using surface streets because the freeways were clogged with rush hour traffic. It was stop and go on Aurora Avenue but still faster than the freeway. It was after five by the time I reached the strip mall and Westover Studios. Alice Kiner was just locking up when I reached the door.

She frowned when she recognized me. "Uncle Myron has already left."

"Actually I wanted to talk with you. I won't hold you up long. Can I buy you a cup of coffee?"

Alice Kiner wasn't exactly your classical beauty; her face was a little too long and her lips a little too thin, but she had that indefinable something that surpasses ordinary beauty. I stared at her trying to discern what it was that made her so unique.

She fiddled with her keys for a minute, then turned back and unlocked the door. "Why don't we talk here."

That wasn't exactly what I had in mind but I was afraid if I refused, she'd just walk out. One advantage the police have over us P.I.s, they're official. Talk here or downtown. Nobody *has* to talk to us.

I'd really have preferred a more casual atmosphere but I waited while she re-locked the door and followed her down the hall to her uncle's office. The love seat was again piled high with proofs and papers, but she swept them into a pile and deposited them on the floor. She took her uncle's chair, folded her hands on the desk, and waited for me to speak.

I felt like a schoolgirl called to the principal's office. I wanted her relaxed but I was the one that was nervous. "That's an incredible portrait in the window. Your uncle has a rare talent."

"Uncle Myron didn't take that picture, Mark did."

I couldn't keep the surprise out of my voice. "Mark Kiner? But it must have been taken years ago." Realizing how that must have sounded, I stuttered, "Sorry. I didn't mean... that is—"

She waved a hand. "Never mind, I know what you mean." A smile, full of love and pride, lit up her face, making her truly beautiful. "Mark was only fifteen when he took that picture. He would have been one of the world's great photographers if things..."

"If he hadn't met Maureen Donlevy? You must hate her very much."

Her smile faded and she leaned forward. "Miss Roarke, what I am going to tell you is strictly between us. If you repeat it to my uncle, I'll deny every word. You see, he loves Mark like a son. He—"

I wanted to hear what she had to say but I couldn't lie to her. "Miss Kiner, if what you tell me has any bearing on the disappearance of Maureen Trent, then I can't promise not to tell the police."

She dismissed that with a wave of her hand. "This has nothing to do with Mrs. Trent. I want to tell you the truth about my brother."

She leaned back in the chair. Her gaze drifted over me and settled on a point on the wall behind me. "You're right. Mark does have a unique talent. Without a camera, he's like a blind man but... but with a viewfinder, he can make the camera see right into the soul of a person. With a camera, he can strip away veneer, all the protective coverings we hide behind. It's not something everyone can appreciate. Some even resent it, are frightened by being so exposed."

She looked back at me. "No, Miss Roarke, I don't hate Maureen. If anything I pity her." She stood up and moved around the desk. "Wait here."

She left the room, returning a few minutes later with a large accordion folder. Slipping the elastic band free, she selected several photographs and laid them, face down, on the desk.

She picked up one, looked at it for a moment, then handed to me. "This is the first photograph Mark took of Maureen."

At first glance it appeared to be an ordinary headshot, but as I studied it, I knew I was seeing something special. It was almost as if two pictures had been superimposed; one an angry, greedy woman, the other a shy, hesitant, very frightened child.

I laid it on the desk as Alice handed me another photo, back side towards me. Scribbled at the top was a date. It had been taken several years previously.

"This was the second portrait," she said, "taken shortly before they began living together."

I turned it over and the hairs on the back of my neck quivered. In this one the feeling of anger was intensified, the jaw had firmed, the eyes contemptuous and determined, but behind the arrogance was still a very bewildered, frightened child. It was a picture of a soul in torment.

She picked up the last photo and held it for a moment. "This was Mark's last portrait of her, taken a few days before she left him."

I wasn't sure I wanted to see it but I took it anyway. It was a pose similar to the one Ian Donlevy had given me, but oh, so different. Through an opaque veneer of sophistication churned incipient madness. The child had disappeared.

I laid it on the desk with the other two photographs and looked at Alice. I knew she could see the horror in my face, for I couldn't hide it. It was trick photography. It had to be.

Alice, as if she had read my mind, smiled gently. "No tricks. Now you understand why I said I pitied her."

I licked my lips and swallowed. "But she destroyed your brother."

She shook her head. "Maureen didn't destroy Mark, his talent destroyed him. He couldn't face what he was able to capture with the camera."

She gathered up the pictures and stuffed them back in the folder. "It wasn't just Maureen. If you saw the rest of these photographs, you'd understand. I can't show them to you because you might recognize some of them and it wouldn't be fair. I can only tell you that they are all the same. They all show the person behind the mask."

She slid the elastic back in place. "We all have our secret selves, ones we keep hidden from the world, sometimes even from ourselves."

"But not everyone is mad or evil," I protested.

"Of course not. People hide all kinds of things, some little, some big. We hide our fears, our insecurities, our goodness as well as our greed, hate, or anger. We all present some kind of mask to the world. That's what Mark could never understand or accept. It's why he hides behind alcohol and drugs."

She tapped the folder. "Maureen didn't destroy Mark. He saw her as she really was when he developed that first negative."

"What about the money she took?"

"Money has never meant much to Mark. I think he knew from the start what she would do. He told me once that money was Maureen's security blanket. Almost everyone needs some kind of security blanket. That's why he refused to sell our parents' home. It's his security blanket. He understood her and loved her anyway. As much as his drugs allowed him to love anyone."

I won't deny that what Alice had told me and the photos she had shown me shook me up. I wondered what a Mark Kiner portrait of me would show. Alice was right. We all wear public masks. I didn't want mine exposed, even to myself.

What I did want was fresh air and sanity. If Maureen was mad, so was Mark Kiner. Maybe Alice, too. Who knew what she might be hiding behind that gentle smile. I stood up, waited for her to put away the file and unlock the door, then made a beeline for my car.

It was raining again but the traffic had eased. I cut across to Interstate 5, then crossed the Evergreen Point Bridge and took 405 to Interstate 90. I pushed the speed limit, wanting to get home. Wanting, needing the safety and security of my own home.

The smell of cooking that greeted me as I opened the kitchen door lightened my mood. Carmen gave me a big smile. "I make cheese enchiladas. You better hurry. Your friends will be here soon."

Her words stopped me in my tracks. Then I remembered and groaned. It was the first Tuesday of the month and my turn to host our rehearsals. I hadn't touched my recorder in over a week.

I dashed upstairs, took a quick shower, and threw on a hostess gown. Back downstairs, I gave the living room a hasty glance, but I needn't have worried. Carmen had the chairs and music stands arranged. I ate in the kitchen, while Carmen worked around me, preparing a light snack to be served after our practice.

I'd barely finished eating when the dogs announced the arrival of a car. I shushed them and got them corralled in the den just in time to answer the doorbell.

Andy McManus and Nathan Blumberg trooped in, Melissa Corning trailing behind, all carrying their instrument cases and music scores. Andy is a big man, over six feet tall, with broad shoulders, a heavy body, and large hands. The last person you would expect to play the flute. He looks more like a truck driver than an eye surgeon. And he's one hell of a lover. We'd had a brief but passionate affair that had graduated to a strong friendship.

Melissa is a lot like Mary Sue in appearance, small and dainty. The similarity ended there. Mary Sue is outgoing and vibrant. Melissa is introverted and, well for want of a better word, prissy. She plays the viol.

Nathan Blumberg, with his slender build, slightly hunched shoulders and thick glasses looks like what he is—an accountant. Which is a shame because his talent for the violin is magical. If he'd had the same training and encouragement, he'd be every bit as good as Itzak Perlman.

I brought out the music I'd purchased in Boston. It created as much excitement among the group as I'd anticipated and it was nearly an hour before we settled down to serious practice.

It was a wonderful evening, just what I needed to pull myself out of the doldrums. Perhaps music is my security blanket. By the time they had packed up their instruments and left, I was more relaxed than I'd been since Ian Donlevy had come to my office.

I let the dogs out, picked up the dirty cups and crumpled napkins, then straightened the room. After letting the dogs in, I checked the doors and windows and went to bed without once thinking about the case.

A weak sun was painting the tops of the mountains with a pastel brush when I went for my usual ride the next morning. I spent a half hour with Julio discussing the horses, then worked out on the Nautilus for another half hour before showering and dressing. I was just finishing breakfast when Ian Donlevy called and asked me to meet him at a restaurant at the Ballard locks for lunch.

I added the notes on my conversation with Alice Kiner to the file, then called Angela Bottoms. I still wanted to see Claudia Oliver. Angela agreed to contact Claudia and try to set up an appointment. I told her to leave a message on my answering machine. I also called an attorney friend. He didn't know Anson Penman personally but said he'd ask around and let me know what he found out. I spent another hour paying bills and taking care of personal correspondence.

I tried to reach Sam but he was out of the office. I wanted to know why he hadn't told me he'd been assigned to the case and was anxious to compare notes. I left a message asking him to call me.

I still hadn't checked out Tree Alert. Their address was in the University district. I'd have time to stop by on my way to Ballard.

Carmen caught me on the way out, wanting to know when I would like to have Mom and Sam McCready to dinner. Carmen loves for me to entertain. It gives her a chance to show off her cooking skills. "Sorry," I said. "It'll have to wait until I finish this case."

She looked so disappointed, I added, "As soon as I'm free,

I'll throw a big party."

"Dinner party?"

"Dinner party, and not just for Mom and Sam. A big party. I promise." I left her grinning happily.

The Tree Alert office wasn't hard to find but a parking place was. I finally parked in the Meany Towers Hotel parking lot, hoping they wouldn't tow my car away.

Tree Alert's reception area was considerably more upscale than Clean Sweep. It's green wall-to-wall carpet blended nicely with the lighter green wallpaper and the huge photographs of forest scenes that decorated the walls. An L-shaped metal desk with a matching credenza behind it sat between two windows.

A tiny bird of a woman, white-haired and wearing a pair of John Lennon glasses glanced up as I crossed the room. Shoving the glasses down on her long, slender nose with one finger, she peered over them. Her "may I help you" in a high voice accentuated her bird-like appearance.

I introduced myself and handed her my card.

She studied it for a moment, then laid it on the desk and looked back at me, wariness clouding her eyes. "Are you sure you have the right office?"

I nodded. "I'm here about Maureen Trent. I understand she is a member of your organization. I'd like to talk to someone who knew her."

"What about?" Her tone was definitely defensive.

"She's missing. I've been hired to find her."

She hesitated, studying me intently.

I tried to recall some of the newspaper stories about Tree Alert. Not all of their activities had been strictly legal. If I remembered correctly, at least two of their members were currently serving jail terms for spiking trees.

I took a deep breath. "I'm not investigating your organization. I just need to talk with those who might know of her other interests or something she might have said that would give me more ideas on where to look or other people to talk to."

She continued to stare at me, then stood up and moved out from behind her desk. "Wait here." She left the room and I waited. And waited. And waited.

I was beginning to wonder if she'd done a bunk when the door finally opened and she motioned, saying, "If you'll come with me, some of our members have agreed to talk to you."

She led me down a short hall past a couple of closed door and into a large room with long tables stretching end to end down the center and covered with stacks of paper, boxes of envelopes, a postage meter and other paraphernalia. A row of file cabinets lined one wall; stacks of cartons and piles of posters and flyers were heaped under the windows.

Half a dozen people ranging in age from early teens to pensioners were busily addressing and stuffing envelopes. The bird-lady introduced me, then took a seat at the end of the table.

I questioned them for nearly an hour but it didn't put me any further ahead in my search for Maureen Trent. They all knew her but no one had seen her for a couple of months. No one seemed to think that was significant since their current activities were limited to bombarding elected officials with letters. They all appeared genuinely shocked to hear of her disappearance. No one had noticed anything strange about her behavior. No one had any idea where she might have gone. No one knew anything about her activities, social or otherwise, outside their own group.

I collected my car and headed on out to Ballard.   Ian

Donlevy was seated at a window table nursing a gin and tonic when I arrived at the restaurant. There were new lines around his mouth and his eyes had lost some of their brightness but he was still a handsome man. I had to repress the little tingle of excitement that raced down my spine as I took the seat across from him. Under better circumstances, I could go for him in a big way.

"What did you find out in Boston?" he asked after we'd ordered.

I gave him a rundown of my meeting with Seth Steiner then asked him about Anson Penman.

He shook his head, obviously not interested in the attorney. "Maureen never mentioned him. Look, Kerry... may I call you Kerry? I want you–"

The waitress brought out food and when she left I waited for him to continue, but he'd didn't. We ate in silence. When we'd finished, Ian signaled the waitress who took away our plates and brought coffee.

Finally, he said, "I can't believe Arthur killed Maureen." He'd been staring out the window, although I doubt he was really seeing the passing parade of boats entering and leaving the locks. Now he turned to look at me. "Do you think she's dead?" I didn't know what to say. His gaze locked with mine, and whether he wanted to hear it or not, I had to answer truthfully. The word stuck in my throat but I finally got it out in a harsh whisper. "Yes."

Ian's face took on a gray tinge and the lines around his mouth deepened. I wanted to withdraw the word but I couldn't. I truly believed in my heart that Maureen Trent was dead.

He pulled himself together and asked, "Do you think Arthur killed her?"

"I don't know." I hesitated, not sure how he would take

the request I was about to make. "I need to know more about your sister's finances. Can you find out if she or Arthur have made any large withdrawals in the last few weeks?"

His eyes widened. "You think she's been kidnapped?"

Actually, that wasn't what I was thinking but I didn't say so. "It's always a possibility. One that should be checked out."

He nodded. "I'll go by Arthur's this evening and go through his desk."

"If your sister had a separate account, would you check it, too?" I rushed on before he could respond. "There's something else. It may mean absolutely nothing but..."

I took a deep breath and plunged ahead, telling him about Buffy's disappearance. I went on to tell him what I'd learned about Marie Brill and Abigail Steiner. "I know it sounds crazy, but what if there is a connection?"

I waited for him to make a sarcastic reply but he didn't. He didn't say anything, just turned his head and stared out the window while my nerves tightened like violin strings. At last he looked back at me. "Do *you* believe there's a connection?"

"I don't know. It seems pretty far-fetched even to me but..." I shrugged.

He played with the handle of coffee cup, picked up a spoon and stirred his coffee, tapped the spoon on the table, and finally, without looking up, said, "I want to know about Arthur's first marriage, whether he ever got a divorce. You'd have to go to California to find out?"

"I could check the records by mail but it would take a long time."

He shook his head. "No. Go to California." He looked up. "While you're there you could check on these other women, couldn't you?"

"Yes, but it would take a lot of time and cost a lot of

money."

He dropped the spoon he'd been playing with, sat back and took out his checkbook. He scribbled a check, tore it out, and tossed it across the table. "Can you fly to Los Angeles this afternoon?"

I picked up the check, glanced at it, and almost choked. There was nothing niggardly about him. "Yes, if I can get a flight."

"Fine. Call me every couple of days."

He opened the leather folder, glanced at the lunch check, tossed a few bills on top, closed it, and stood up. His lips twitched into what I assumed was meant to be a smile, said, "Good luck," and walked out.

I folded his check, stuffed it in my purse and left. He was pulling out of the parking lot by the time I got outside. It didn't surprise me to see he was driving a silver gray Jaguar.

I drove to my office. The red light was flashing on my answering machine. Before listening to the messages, I called Alaska Airlines and booked a seat on an evening flight to Los Angeles, then called Budget Car Rental and reserved a Lincoln TownCar. I had a feeling I was going to be doing a lot of driving and I like my creature comforts.

I turned on the answering machine and listened to the messages. The first call was from a guy I'd dated a couple of times, which was two too many, the second was from Angela Bottoms saying that Claudia Oliver would meet me at five-fifteen at a chicken joint in South Seattle. I wondered how we were supposed to know each other.

The next call was from my attorney friend. My ears perked up as I listened to Bernie saying, "Kerry, I don't know what was the matter with me this morning. I should have recognized Penman's name right away. I've met him a couple of times at bar association meetings. I hear he's going to run for city counsel. He's got a lot of support among the minorities and he has political ambitions. He's a so-so attorney. Does very little trial work, has a few private clients that pay the rent, does a lot of pro bono work for the homeless and volunteers his services for a lot of politically correct causes. I believe both his father and mother were doctors. If I remember correctly, they died in a plane crash a few years ago and Penman supposedly came into a good-sized inheritance. If you need more information, give me a call and I'll see what I can dig up."

If Anson Penman was politically ambitious and was having an affair with Maureen Trent, no wonder he was nervous.

I listened in surprise to the last call: a nervous Seth Steiner apologizing for his "descent into the arms of Bacchus" and hoping I would forgive any inappropriate actions because he'd "brandied too heartily" and hoped I'd overlook his drink-induced rambling. His call did nothing to raise him in my estimation. I still thought he was a pompous bore, and I couldn't help wondering if his call was meant to obscure any concern raised by his comments and actions.

I erased the tape, reset the machine, and called Carmen, telling her I was going out of town for an extended time and asking her to pack a case for me and have Julio bring it to the airport. I checked through my mail, paid a few office bills, and made out a deposit slip for the check Ian Donlevy had given me. Stopping by my bank on my way to meet Claudia Oliver, I deposited Donlevy's check and collected cash for the trip.

Mine was the only white face in the restaurant, but I didn't let it bother me. It wasn't the first time my job had taken me to ethnic spots and it probably wouldn't be the last. I ordered their snack basket and a large Coke. Carrying the drink in its

110

paper cup, I settled into a booth in back, lit a cigarette and waited. I might not know Claudia but she would have no trouble finding me.

I needn't have worried. I recognized her the minute she walked in the door. Perhaps I shouldn't have been surprised, but I was. Claudia Oliver was Anson Penman's secretary.

CHAPTER ELEVEN

The last time I'd seen Claudia Oliver, she'd been slipping back behind her desk in Anson Penman's office. I'd assumed at the time that she had been eavesdropping, now I was sure she'd been doing exactly that. She glanced around the room, spotted me, and walked over. There was no friendliness in her face as she slid into the booth across from me, or in her voice as she said, "You wanted to see me."

"Yes. I understand you and Maureen Trent worked together at Clean Sweep. When was the last time you saw her?"

A black girl in her teens gave the table a half-hearted swipe with a damp towel and deposited a plastic basket with two pieces of chicken and a biscuit in front of me.

Claudia waited until the girl, moving to some rhythm only she could hear, had jiggled back behind the counter, before she answered. "I already told the police all I know. Whatever that white bitch said, it was a lie."

"What makes you think she said anything?"

"Why else you be coming around bothering Mr. Penman? That woman's just trying to make trouble."

"What trouble could she make?"

She glared at me. "You know. You helping her, ain't you? Coming around trying to put pressure on him. You don't fool me none, girl."

"I'm not pressuring anyone. I just want to know about the

last time you saw Maureen Trent. You told the police that the two of you were the last to leave the meeting. What time was that?"

"A few minutes after nine o'clock, maybe ten after."

"Who else was at the meeting?"

She rattled off a few names and I scribbled them on a napkin. When I got back from California, I'd check them out. "Why were you two the last to leave?"

"Angela had to leave early and I said I'd close up. Trent went to the rest room and I had to wait for her to come out to lock up."

"Did she mention anything about her plans?"

"You gotta be kiddin'. No way that stuck up whitey bitch would tell me diddly. She didn't say a word, just strutted on down the stairs and up the street."

"Was anyone waiting for her or did she meet anyone?"

"Whatever she told you, it was a lie. Mr. Penman went straight home."

"Why do you say that? Was she in the habit of meeting Penman? Did they have a social relationship?"

"Huh. As if you didn't know! She'd been coming on to him for months but he wasn't interested in no white pussy. If she got herself knocked up, it wasn't by Anson, no matter what she says."

"Did they meet, other than at Clean Sweep?"

"She came to the office a few times."

"She didn't meet him that night?"

"That's what I said. He went straight home."

"How do you know?"

She bit her lip and looked away. "'Cause he'd forgotten some papers. I took them by his house. He was home." She turned back and met my gaze. "Alone."

I'd definitely look into Anson Penman when I got back.

"So you saw no one on the street?"

"Just the usual."

"Usual?"

"Street people. They always around."

"No one followed her, spoke to her?"

"Nah. There was some old man walking up the street behind her but he was just a bum."

"What did he look like?"

She shrugged. "Just an old man. I only saw him from the back. Kinda skinny, not too tall, wearing one of those flat caps. Just another homeless man."

"You told the police you weren't surprised when Mrs. Trent missed two meetings. Why not? Had she missed other meetings?"

"No. She always came, always had her say."

"But you weren't surprised when she stopped coming."

"I figured she was bored. Angela always let her talk but there wasn't no way we were going to agree to no picketing and marching and all the things she wanted to do."

"Mrs. Trent seemed perfectly normal that evening? No nervous mannerisms, nothing unusual in her behavior?"

Claudia's eyes narrowed. "You ain't jivin' me? She really has disappeared? This ain't no shit?"

"She really is missing. As far as we know, the last time she was seen was at a dry cleaners about nine in the morning on the nineteenth."

"You ain't shittin' me?"

"I ain't shittin' you. Are you sure there's nothing you can tell me?"

Claudia leaned back in her chair, her gaze raking my face. After a moment, she leaned forward and said, "I don't know if it means anything, but she didn't have much of anything to say that night. Mostly she just sat there with a blank look on her face, like she was bored outta her skull. I figured she was getting ready to dump us. That's why I wasn't surprised she never came back."

"Bored or was she concentrating on something else?"

Claudia shrugged. "How should I know?"

"When she left, she just walked up the street? She didn't talk to anyone?"

"Nah. She did look over her shoulder a couple of times, but she didn't stop." Claudia stood up. "That's all I got to say, 'cept you stop bothering Mr. Penman. He didn't have nuthin' to do with that stuck-up bitch."

I watched her walk out then turned my attention to the chicken. Even cold, it was delicious and the biscuit even fluffier than those Carmen made. A hell of a lot better than what they'd be serving on the plane.

On the drive to the airport, I pondered Claudia's comments about Anson Penman and Maureen Trent. Why had Maureen gone to Penman's office? Clean Sweep business or something else? Was there a personal relationship between the two of them or was Claudia simply jealous? That she was in love with her boss was obvious in the way her eyes softened and the tone of her voice when she spoke his name.

Julio was waiting at the ticket counter when I got to the airport. I collected my suitcase from him, bought my ticket, and headed for the gate. From a pay phone, I called Mary Sue, told her I was on my way to Los Angeles, and dictated a report on my afternoon contacts.

I spent the flight bringing my notes up to date, then reading and re-reading the file in an effort to discourage my garrulous seat mate. It didn't help. Nor did my refusing the drinks he tried to buy me. He followed me off the plane, still trying to get me to have dinner with him. I finally lost him in the bustle at the baggage claim area.

After the crispness of Seattle, I found the warm, sultry, smog-laden air of Los Angeles suffocating. By the time I'd located my rental car and headed down Century Boulevard, my eyes were watering and my throat burning.

Los Angeles is not my favorite city and the freeway system drives me crazy. I'd rather tackle a one-lane mountain road in pea soup fog than drive in Los Angeles traffic. I took the San Diego Freeway to the Santa Monica, then got in the wrong lane and ended up on the Harbor Freeway, switched to the Santa Ana and finally ended up where I wanted to be, heading east on the San Bernardino Freeway.

By the time I got to El Monte and found a motel, my head was splitting, my hands aching from gripping the wheel and my shoulder and neck muscles were tied in knots. I wanted nothing so much as a long hot soak in a Jacuzzi. I had to settle for the tub with lukewarm water and bed, making do with those pint-sized pillows motels and hotels are so fond of.

There were a slew of Montgomerys in the phone book, but only five in the El Monte area. I thought about calling, but if Belinda's parents didn't want to talk to me, it's a lot easier to hang up the phone than slam a door in my face. Assuming, of course, that the Montgomery I wanted was still in the area.

I found a AAA office, got a map of California and one of the Los Angeles area, then hunted up a Denny's, had a big breakfast and started my search.

The first address was a rundown apartment building and the man who answered my knock had to be least a hundred years old. He'd never heard of Belinda Montgomery but was more than willing to tell me about his Aunt Melinda and the

116

rest of his family tree. If I hadn't been on a case, I'd have enjoyed listening to him. Some of the anecdotes were interesting. It took me a while to get away from him.

The second address was on a street of old frame bungalows built in the thirties in a neighborhood beginning to decay. It was a quiet, working class neighborhood and the only signs of life were the humming of insects and a fat yellow cat strolling across the street. The house had been recently painted and the lawn was neater than most of the others on the block. No one was home.

I struck out at the other three addresses. None of the women I talked to had ever heard of Belinda. It was after three by the time I'd hit all five addresses so I ate a late lunch, drove back to the motel, and took a nap.

At six o'clock I went back to the second address. I could hear music and the murmur of voices as I drove down the street. My nose twitched as the scent of barbecue fought the acrid stench of hot asphalt, exhaust fumes and hot rubber from the millions of automobiles.

There were no lights in the Montgomery house and no one answered my knock. I could hear voices so I followed a brick walk around the side of the house. The back yard was empty; the voices I heard were coming from the next yard. I leaned over the low redwood fence and called out, "Hello. I'm looking for the Montgomerys."

Two middle-aged couples were grouped around a barbecue. They all looked up at my announcement. A chubby little man with a fringe of gray hair strolled over to the fence, a long handled fork clutched in his hand. He smiled but there was a wariness in his eyes. "Were they expecting you?"

"No. I'm in town on business and hoped to squeeze in a quick visit. Will they be home soon?"

The wariness had turned to suspicion. "Known them long?" he asked.

"Actually, I've never met them. A friend of mine in Seattle asked me to stop by and see how they were."

"Your friend have a name?"

"Arthur Trent. Will they be home soon? If so, I'll wait."

Something flickered in his eyes but it was too dark for me to tell what. "They're out of town. Visiting their daughter in Chicago. Won't be back until Sunday."

His words stunned me. I thanked him and walked back to my car. Belinda/Buffy was alive and in touch with her parents. In a way I was relieved. At least Arthur Trent wasn't a modern day Bluebeard. But was he a bigamist?

I drove back to the motel considering where I was going from here. I still wanted to talk to the Montgomerys but I didn't really want to hang around Los Angeles for the next three days. I pulled into the parking space in front of my room, collected the California map I'd picked up that morning and went inside.

Tossing my purse on the dresser, I opened the map on the bed and studied it. The inch or so of Arizona along the border caught my eye, the name Yuma standing out in dark letters. Marriage licenses could be faked. Neither Elliot Brill nor Seth Steiner had said anything about attending the wedding. I might as well check it out. It was only a little after seven and my afternoon nap had left me wide-awake. I could be in Yuma by midnight.

I folded the map and got up. I hadn't bothered to unpack the night before so it was only a matter of tossing a few things in my suitcase and checking out. Fifteen minutes later I was on the San Bernardino Freeway heading east towards Indio.

I stopped for coffee in Indio and it's a good thing I did

because I needed to be wide awake, with all my wits about me, for the next eighty-odd miles. Once past the little town of Thermal, with its rows of date palms marching like soldiers across the desert, there was nothing but sand, rock, and sagebrush. The road south was a two-lane strip of asphalt full of dips, narrow bridges, and tractor-trailers that paid no attention to the speed limit.

On my left the Salton Sea lay like a lake of ebony tar. I passed a sign informing me that Salton City was somewhere along the shore but only a couple of lights twinkled like fireflies in the darkness to lend it credence. I passed an overturned flatbed trailer, its load of baled hay tumbled along the side of the road, barely missed hitting a jack rabbit, did run over a snake, and was nearly run off the road twice by impatient drivers.

The sagebrush finally gave way to irrigated fields and then my headlights picked out a 25 MPH sign and a WELCOME TO WESTMORLAND sign. They also picked up a reflection off something shiny partially hidden by the sign and brush. Not taking any chances, I hit the brakes. It wouldn't be the first small town I'd come across that swelled its coffers with speeding fines. I grinned as the police car pulled in behind me and followed me through town at a stately 22 MPH.

I kept my speed down all the way through the towns of Brawley and El Centro, found Interstate 8, and drove the final sixty miles to Yuma. The town didn't impress me but maybe it would look better in daylight.

I left the interstate and cruised down Fourth Street. There didn't seem to be a central district. The town had obviously grown up along this one street. I found the Stardust Motel, checked in, and went hunting for food. I was so hungry I could have eaten anything, up to and including rattlesnake. Their dining room was closing, but I talked them into fixing me a couple of roast beef sandwiches to take to my room, collected a Coke from the machine and made do. Tomorrow I'd find the best restaurant in town and eat my fill.

Daylight didn't improve the town. It still struck me as dirty and unattractive. Perhaps it was the blowing dust that coated everything, perhaps the lack of trees and grass, perhaps the depressing shades of beige and gray. Whatever my feelings, it obviously appealed to a lot of people. The traffic was almost as bad as Seattle, and at least half the cars had out of state license plates, a lot from my home state of Washington, with a goodly number from Idaho and Montana and a plethora of Canadian plates.

I found a Denny's Restaurant and ordered a Grand Slam Breakfast. When I'd satisfied the inner woman, I hunted up the Chamber of Commerce. The clerk was friendly, a little too friendly, because I had to listen to a spiel on the delights to be found in the Yuma area. If I'd been interested in baseball spring training or golf or the myriad RV parks offered, it might have been helpful. She finally agreed that, indeed there was a wedding chapel, and I had to listen to a recitation of the charming weddings that had been performed there over the donkey's years it had been in business. I finally got the address and directions and got out of there.

When I found the place, I could well believe it had been in business for years. I could also believe that woman who answered my ring had assisted at the first wedding.

I had a story all ready, but I didn't need it. A fifty-dollar bill convinced her to dig out her old records. When I drove back to the motel, I had a copy of the marriage license issued to Belinda Eileen Montgomery, spinster, age 18 of El Monte, California and Arthur Dennis Trent, bachelor, age 26 of Long

Beach, California. I also had a copy of the marriage certificate dated July 22, 1979. Arthur Trent had indeed married Belinda. But had he gotten a divorce?

CHAPTER TWELVE

I drove back to the motel, trying to decide what to do next. It was reasonable to suppose that if Arthur Trent had filed for divorce, it would have been in Los Angeles County but it was just that, a supposition. I had no idea where Arthur and Belinda/Buffy had lived during their marriage. It could just as easily have been Orange or any of the other neighboring counties. It was already noon on Friday. By the time I drove back to L.A., all of the county offices would be closed. I debated turning in the car and flying back to Seattle. The temperature was in the nineties and I hate heat.

Instead, I thought about San Diego only a hundred and fifty miles away. The fourth Boatnik was in San Diego. What was his name? Lockman. Dale Lockman. Had he known Belinda/Buffy? Had he been around when she disappeared? Besides, I was still curious as to why the four fast friends had split up. Why none of them wanted to talk about it.

I couldn't face driving across the desert in the heat of the day even in the air conditioned Lincoln. I stopped at a boutique to pick up a bathing suit and sunglasses and spent the afternoon in the pool. It beat sitting in a stuffy room. Every few minutes, I'd swim a dozen laps to cool off. I would at least return home with the beginnings of a tan, something to show for my efforts. So far I didn't have much else.

By the time the sun was sinking behind the Laguna Mountains, I'd checked out and was heading west on Interstate

8. It was nearly ten when I got to San Diego and a brisk breeze was blowing in from the ocean. Wanting to be near the water, I checked into the Bahia Hotel on Mission Bay. I was tired but my mind was spinning faster than a roulette wheel. I opened the drapes and looked out at the water. The three quarters moon cast ribbons of silver across the bay. Smog isn't so bad in San Diego, although it's coming. It won't be long before it's as thick as in L.A.

I needed air and exercise to unwind. I could feel my muscles turning to mush. When I got home, I'd really have to work out on the Nautilus and NordicTrack.

I pulled a sweat suit out of the suitcase and a pair of Reeboks, changed, and walked down three flights of stairs and out a side door. Jogging is really not my thing. It's hard on the feet and joints but it's better than nothing. I trotted what felt like half way around the bay, then back, sucking in the cool ocean air, feeling it wash away the poisons from my lungs. Back in my room, I stripped and fell into bed, naked and sweaty, and was asleep before I could pull up the blanket.

I awoke sometime later thoroughly chilled, my heart racing. I could remember little of the nightmare except that I was naked on Mt. Rainier, being chased through the snow by a faceless beggar who kept hitting me across the back with an oar and giggling hysterically.

I drew a bath, making the water as hot as I could stand it. By the time the chill had begun to leave my bones, the dream had faded and I was relaxed and sleepy. I slipped into a nightgown and went back to bed. This time I pulled up the blankets.

When I awoke Saturday morning, the morning fog still swirled over the bay. I spent a few minutes staring out at the vague outlines of the building across the bay and breathing the cool, moist air. It was still very early but I was wide-awake and anxious to get on with finding the fourth Boatnik. I made myself a cup of the instant coffee provided by the hotel and picked up the phone book. There was no Dale or D. Lockman listed. Finding him wasn't going to be easy. I turned to Marinas and began a list. I had a feeling it was going to be a long day. There were a lot of marinas and boat yards in the area.

I unpacked, took a quick shower and slipped into a pair of beige gabardine slacks, matching silk blouse, added a yellow print scarf and went downstairs for my usual big breakfast. I'd need all my energy for the search.

I started at Quivara Basin because it was the closest, then worked south hitting every marina and boat yard all the way south of Chula Vista, then back north to La Jolla. Boating is as popular in San Diego as it is in Puget Sound.

I must have talked to two hundred boat owners and marina personnel before I finally picked up a lead. The owner of a sixty-foot sloop I was admiring thought he remembered a Lockman working for a marine outfitter. He gave me the name and address of the company and directions.

I only got lost once before I found it. It was locked up tighter than a drum. I was writing down the emergency numbers posted on a card in the window when a young man wearing cutoffs, canvas deck shoes, a baseball cap and nothing else came around the side of the building. He was gorgeous and there was something in his body movements and the way his gaze wandered over my body that shouted sex-sex-sex. With his blue eyes, thick blond hair and muscular physique, he could have posed for Play Girl or a centerfold in Cosmopolitan. I couldn't help wondering if his fantastic tan extended all the way. Too bad he was so young. I haven't stooped to cradle robbing, but he was tempting. Very tempting.

His, "Sorry, Ma'am, we're closed," made me feel old. I'm not ready to be called Ma'am yet. That's how people address my mother.

Still, he had an enchanting smile and I found my lips responding. "I'm trying to locate Dale Lockman. I understand he works here."

The smile disappeared. "You a reporter?"

"No. I'm from Seattle. A mutual friend suggested I look him up. Will he be in tomorrow?"

"Nope. He don't work here regular."

I let my disappointment show. "I was looking forward to meeting him but I was planning to go home tomorrow night." I started to turn away, then stopped. "You don't know where he lives, do you? Perhaps I could catch him at home."

"Last I heard, he had a room down on G Street. You'd have better luck catching him at the Dolphin Inn; it's a bar down on Market Street. He hangs out there most of the time these days."

I hesitated. "How would I know him?"

"Oh, you can't miss him. He's over six feet, about one ninety, blond hair."

"That could describe a lot of men, including you."

The grin was back. "Yeah, but I don't have an ugly scar down the left side of my face."

I thanked him and got back in the car. It was five-thirty, a little too early to go bar hopping. Besides, I'd skipped lunch and was hungry. I drove back to the Bahia, changed into black silk slacks, topped them with a white satin smock and a pair of black flats with steel toes hidden under the satin surface. I'd had them specially made for just such outings. A girl never knows when she might have to protect her virtue.

125

The food in the Bahia dining room was excellent and I took full advantage of it. I'm not much of a drinker and wanted something in my stomach to soak up the liquor I might have to drink before I found Dale Lockman.

I needn't have worried. I spotted him as soon as I walked in the Dolphin and my eyes adjusted to the gloom. There were perhaps twenty people in the place, mostly older, unshaven men with a few slatternly women but he was alone at the end of the bar, elbows resting on the padded railing. The scar glowed red in the reflection of the beer sign on the wall.

Conversation dwindled and I could feel everyone's eyes on me I crossed the floor. I was definitely overdressed. Lockman continued to stare into the glass in his hand as I slid onto the stool next to him. The bartender walked over and I ordered a Coke. He looked at Lockman, who waved a finger without looking at either of us.

I tossed a five on the bar when he delivered our drinks and said, "On me, and keep the change." He glanced at the man beside me, shrugged, and picked up the bill.

Lockman still didn't look at me so I said, "You are Dale Lockman, aren't you?"

He still didn't turn. "No interviews."

"My name is Kerry Roarke. I'm from Seattle."

The corner of his mouth quirked into a sneer. "A long way to come for a story. No news in Seattle?"

"I need to ask you some questions."

He sipped his drink, ignoring me.

"Mr. Lockman, this is important. Can we go somewhere and talk?"

"We got nothing to talk about. I told you, no interviews."

I pulled out a business card and slid it across the bar. "Look, I don't know what your problem is but your friend,

Arthur Trent, is in trouble and needs your help."

He did look at me then. "You're not a reporter?"

"No. I'm a private detective."

He picked up my card and studied it, then slipped it in his pocket and picked up his drink. "This could be a trick."

"It's not."

He shrugged. "So Art's in trouble. I can't help him. I haven't seen him in almost twenty years."

"I know that but I still need to talk to you. Please. It really is important."

"So ask you questions."

"When was the last time you saw Arthur Trent?"

"The day after we all graduated from college."

"Did you know his wife Belinda?"

"No. I didn't know he had married. Good for him. I hope his marriage worked out better than mine."

It was obvious that he wasn't going to cooperate. I decided to try shock tactics. "Arthur's first wife, Belinda, disappeared several years ago, now his second wife has disappeared. The police believe he killed her"

That did get a reaction, although not the one I was hoping for. He stood up and grabbed my arm, pulling me off the stool. I tried to pull away but his fingers bit into my arm like talons as he hauled me towards the door. I was angry and a little scared but not enough to make a scene.

"Let go, you ass." I was definitely going to have bruises in the morning.

He ignored me until we reached the sidewalk, then he stopped, still gripping my arm. "You got a car?"

"Let go of me."

He eased his grip but didn't let go of my arm. "You wanted to talk. Okay, we'll talk but not in public." He grabbed my purse and let go of me to rummage through it. Coming up with the keys, he handed it back to me. "Where are you parked?"

I glared at him. He examined the rental company tag on the keys, then clamped a hand on my wrist and started down the street. I had to trot to keep up. He spotted the Budget sticker on the back of the car, unlocked the door, and shoved me, none to gently, into the passenger seat. I debated jumping out while he circled the car, but my curiosity was reaching critical mass. Arthur's predicament had obviously shocked him but it was more than that. Something was really bothering him and I wanted to know what it was.

He drove a few blocks then parked in front of an adult bookstore. "Where are we going?" I asked.

"I live upstairs."

I hesitated, wondering what I was getting myself into. He ran his gaze over my body, starting at my feet and working his way up until our glances locked. His upper lip curled. "Relax, you're not my type. If you want to talk, come on. If you don't, take off. Nobody's holding you."

He turned and crossed the sidewalk. I followed him up a set of stairs between the bookstore and a greasy spoon restaurant and down a dim hall. He opened a door and motioned me inside. "It ain't the Waldorf but we'll have privacy."

It was a large room, with a high ceiling and tall windows. A broken-down couch graced one wall, with a cigarette-burn-scarred dresser at one end and a cheap coffee table, it's veneer chipped and peeling, in front. A Formica-topped table with tubular steel legs and two mismatched chairs sat in front of the window. A coffee maker, an electric hot plate and several bottles and jars crowded one end of the table. The other wall was taken up with an unmade bed that sagged in the middle and a forty-year-old refrigerator was jammed in the corner.

He gathered an armload of dirty clothes off the couch and tossed them in the corner. "Have a seat. Want a beer?"

"No, thanks." I sat down and leaned back. A cockroach crawled out from between the cushions, dashed up the back of the couch, and disappeared down the wall. I sat up and inched up to the edge of the couch, as far from the wall as possible. I loathe bugs.

Lockman carried a bottle of Schlitz over to the coffee table, glanced around, picked up an overflowing ashtray from the dresser, emptied it into a paper sack, and slapped it down beside the beer. "Go ahead and smoke."

That surprised me until I remembered he'd rifled through my purse after the car keys. I pulled out the pack of Camel Lights and lit up, beginning to relax.

He swung one of the kitchen chairs around, straddled the seat, leaned an arm across the back, tossed my car keys to me, and reached for the beer. "Okay, Miss Detective-from-Seattle, what's this all about?"

I told him about being hired to find Maureen Trent, how the attempt to verify Arthur's alibi had lead me first to Elliot Brill, then to Seth Steiner. And how I had learned of Arthur's first marriage and Belinda/Buffy's disappearance.

"But apparently she's no longer missing. Her parents are visiting her right now—in Chicago. According to a neighbor, they'll be back tomorrow night. I plan to talk to them then."

"What has all of this to do with me? I haven't seen or talked to any of them in almost twenty years. Hell, I don't think I've even sent a Christmas in the last couple of years, except to Seth."

"I honestly don't know. I was hoping you could tell me. I

think there's more here than meets the eye. I think it has something to do with why the four of you broke up."

"Jesus. Talk about pigeons coming home to roost." He chugged down the rest of the beer, tossed the bottle in the trash sack, and got out another one.

"What really broke up your friendship?"

He pulled a crushed pack of Winston's out of his pocket, selected one, and straightened it with his fingers. He was silent so long I didn't think he was going to answer. "Guilt, I suppose."

Whatever I was expecting, it wasn't that. "Guilt?" I couldn't keep the disbelief out of my voice. "What did you do, cheat on your finals?"

He lit the cigarette, blew out a cloud of smoke, and said, "We killed a woman."

CHAPTER THIRTEEN

I started to laugh. He was pulling my leg. He had to be. "Are you telling me you guys were another Leopold and Loeb? I don't believe..." The laughter died in my throat as he looked up.

His face seemed to have aged ten years and there was a white line around his lips. "No. It wasn't like that. It was an accident."

He stood up and walked to the window. "I've never talked about it, but it's haunted me all these years."

"Maybe talking about it would help."

"Yeah, why not. It can't hurt, not after all this time. To hell with old man Brill." The last sentence was said so low that I wasn't sure I'd heard correctly. Before I could ask him to repeat, he went on.

"What the hell. Not that it will help," he shrugged. "Why not. It was during spring break of our senior year. We'd gone down to San Felipe. Do you know where it is?"

I shook my head then realized he still had his back to me and couldn't see. "No. In Mexico?"

"Yeah. Baja, about a hundred miles south of Calexico. A little fishing village on the Gulf of California. We'd decided to go there because it wasn't as crowded as Ensenada but there were still plenty of chicks and Tecate beer. We really tied one on, stoned out of our minds for most of the week. We were still drunk as skunks when we started back. I don't know how

131

we got across the border without being stopped. God, I wish we had been. A night in the drunk tank would have been peanuts to what happened."

"What did happen?"

"Elliot Brill is the only one that can answer that for sure. Or maybe Seth, he was in the front seat. Elliot was driving, it was his car. His dad had given it to him as an early graduation present. A big black Caddy convertible. Art and I were both in the back, passed out drunk."

He turned and walked back to the chair but didn't sit down. He ran his fingers absently over the back. "The next thing I knew, I was draped over a rock with a broken arm, several busted ribs and my face split open." He ran a finger over the scar. "I remember seeing Art on his back in a manzanita bush. I could hear a woman screaming, then a terrible bang and the whole hillside lit up. I guess I passed out."

He sat down and lit another cigarette. "When I woke up again, I was in the hospital, here in San Diego. Elliot's father's lawyer came to see me. Said Brill would take care of all my medical bills, provide whatever tutoring I needed to graduate with my class and see that no charges were ever brought, if I agreed never to talk about the accident, even to the others."

"You agreed to that?"

He played with his cigarette for a moment without answering. "Yeah. A few hours later, we were all flown in a private jet to a private hospital near San Francisco."

"Never talk about it? You mean you never discussed it with the others?

"No. I guess he offered the same deal to them. We avoided each other as much as possible until graduation. As far as I know, none of us have ever talked about it."

"But you knew a woman had been killed."

"Yeah. That part made the San Diego papers. Somebody sent us each a copy."

"But didn't you feel guilty?"

"Hell, yes, but what could I do? My folks were dirt poor, couldn't even afford to send me spending money. I was on a full scholarship, but I never had two cents to spare. There wasn't anything I could do. Nothing I could have done to prevent the accident. Look, it wasn't my fault. I wasn't driving."

"Didn't the police question you?"

"Once, before I left the hospital here but I couldn't have told them anything, even if I'd wanted to."

"Do you still have the paper?"

"Hell, no! I threw it away."

"Do you know the woman's name?"

He shook his head. "I suppose it was in the paper but I don't remember. You got to understand. I wanted to forget, to put it behind me and get on with my life."

"But you couldn't forget."

He sighed. "No. I still have nightmares. I suppose that's one of the reasons why both my marriages failed. I know Peggy was sick to death of them. They were a lot worse, a lot more frequent, back then. I'd wake up screaming. She wanted me to get help, but of course, I couldn't. I'd have had to talk about the accident and I couldn't do that. Maybe if I'd listened to her, gone to a shrink like she wanted, she'd never have run away."

A cold chill ran down my spine. My mouth was so dry I had to swallow before I could ask, "Your wife left you?"

"Yeah. She went to work one day and never came home. I suppose I should have seen it coming. God knows we'd had

133

enough arguments but I didn't think she was that fed up with our marriage."

"Did she divorce you?"

"No. She just took off. One day she was there, the next she was gone. I never heard from her again. I kept hoping she'd change her mind."

"When did she leave?"

"In the spring of '79."

"So you're still married?"

"No. I divorced her for desertion after I met Corinne."

He stopped speaking and stared at me. His eyes narrowed. I could feel the rage building in him, electrifying the air between us. The hairs on my arms rose. I didn't know what had set him off but this was a dangerous man.

"You bitch. You've really done your homework." The words were spoken slowly, more frightening for their very softness.

He stood up, making an obvious effort to control himself, and got another beer from the refrigerator. I picked up my purse, clutching it in my lap, wondering what was coming next.

He sipped the beer without taking his eyes from me. "That's really what you want to know about, isn't it? You want to know about Corinne. You *are* a goddamned reporter!"

"Mr. Lockman, I don't know the first thing about Corinne. I'd never heard the name until you mentioned it."

"Bull shit!" He slammed down the beer, stalked around the coffee table, and grabbed my wrist, jerking me up. "Get your fancy ass out of here before I throw you out."

He shoved me towards the door. I stumbled, tugged my wrist loose and backed away. "Mr. Lockman–"

"Shut up and get out."

He raised a fist and shook it at me. Steel tipped shoes

wouldn't help me here. I did the only sensible thing.
I ran.

CHAPTER FOURTEEN

I dashed for the door, whipped it open, and ran down the hall. At the foot of the stairs, I glanced up. He hadn't followed me, but I was taking no chances. I scrambled into the car and laid a streak of rubber as I took off.

In the movies all detectives carry guns. I have one, bought when I first got my license. It's locked away in my safe at home. It's never been fired except on the range. The situation with Dale Lockman is one of the reasons I don't carry one. As scared as I was, I'd probably have pulled it and one of us could have been dead. Probably me.

I was still shaken when I got back to the hotel. I wanted a shoulder to cry on, preferably a strong, masculine one. The only person who would understand was Sam McCready. I picked up the phone, hesitated, then dialed Ian Donlevy instead. I couldn't cry on his shoulder but I could make a report.

I told him about the Montgomerys and my trip to Yuma.

"What do you plan to do now?" he asked.

"Tomorrow, I'll go back to El Monte. I'm sure Belinda's parents will know whether or not she and Arthur were divorced. If not, I'll try to contact Belinda by phone."

I gave him a much expunged version of my conversation with Dale Lockman. "Once I clear up the divorce matter, I'd like to check into that accident. It shouldn't take me more than another day."

"You think it's important?"

"Yes."

"Well, do what you think is best," he said, sounding depressed.

I hung up, almost as depressed as Donlevy had sounded. The mystery of the Boatniks and their unlucky marriages intrigued me. I couldn't deny that. But I was no nearer finding Maureen Trent than when I started.

The fear and tension generated by my interview with Dale Lockman had left me hungry. I ordered a sandwich and Coke from room service. As soon as it was delivered, I slipped into a robe and brought my notes up to date as I ate. I watched a couple of sitcoms without really taking in any of the dialogue, my mind on what Lockman had and hadn't told me. At least I now knew what had driven the four friends apart. It must have been hell for all of them. Carrying a secret like that, unable to talk about it, would have generated a tremendous amount of stress. No wonder their marriages had failed.

But there was still something missing and I wanted to know what it was. I didn't plan to leave southern California until I found out.

I slept late Sunday morning, went downstairs for a leisurely breakfast, and took my time packing and checking out. Traffic on Interstate-5 was heavy but I made good time until I hit Orange County, then it was slow going.

It was after three when I checked back into the motel in El Monte. I had no idea what time the Montgomerys were expected back from Chicago but I drove by their house in case they'd taken an early flight. There was no one home. I found restaurant specializing in ribs and had a late lunch, killed some more time gassing up the car and having it washed.

Dusk had fallen when I drove back and parked in front of

the house. The house was still dark but I could hear the neighbors in the back yard again. I strolled back and leaned on the fence.

"Hi. Did Mr. and Mrs. Montgomery get back yet?"

"Sure did but they've gone out to dinner. Should be home anytime."

He invited me over for a beer but I declined and went back to the car. I was just crushing out my third cigarette when a dark blue Honda pulled into the driveway. I watched as the man got out and went around the car to help the woman. He glanced several times in my direction as he assisted her up the walk. I waited until he had the door open before I got out and crossed the lawn.

He turned to face me, blocking the door with his body as I approached. His wife had turned on an inside light and in the reflection I could see that he was in his sixties. He was a big man and had been strong at one time but I guessed most of the muscle had turned to fat.

"Hello," I said, extending my hand, "I'm Kerry Roarke. May I speak to you for a moment?"

He stared at my hand without giving an inch, then took it reluctantly. "Curtis Montgomery. Whatever you're selling, we're not interested."

I handed him my card. "I'm not selling, just looking for information. I'm hoping you can help me."

He tilted the card into the light to read it. His glance had sharpened when he looked back at me. "What's this about?"

"I'm looking for the parents of Belinda Montgomery."

There was a gasp and a moan from behind him. He whirled, surprisingly fast for a man of his size and age, and caught the woman as her knees buckled. She must have weighed at least a hundred and seventy pounds but he carried her across the room as if she weighed no more than a feather. Maybe all that bulk wasn't fat.

The front door opened directly into the living room and I followed him inside as he laid her gently on the couch. He gave me an angry glance and snapped, "Close the door," as he hurried out of the room. I shut the door and knelt beside the woman, chafing her cold hands. I heard water running and a moment later he reappeared with a pill bottle and damp cloth.

Her eyelids were already flickering as he laid the cloth on her forehead. She shoved it away and struggled to sit up.

"Hand me those pillows," he said.

He lifted her shoulders and I shoved the two throw pillows under her head and shoulders. Her eyes opened for a moment and she murmured something I didn't catch. He popped the lid off the bottle, shook out a small glass bottle, and unscrewed the cap. I recognized the tiny white pill he placed under her tongue. Nitroglycerin. I hadn't meant to give the poor woman a heart attack.

I stayed kneeling on the floor, although my right leg was beginning to cramp, until the pain lines on her face eased and her eyes opened again. Then I stood and backed away. She glanced at me then whispered something I couldn't hear.

Curtis Montgomery straightened, tossed the damp rag on the end table and arranged an afghan over her legs, then turned to me. He gestured towards a chair at a right angle to the couch. "Better sit down." He pulled up another chair. "Now, what do you know about our daughter? Do you know where she is, what happened to her?"

"But I thought you just visited her in Chicago?"

The expectancy died out of his face. "We visited Bonita, our younger daughter. We haven't heard from Belinda since she disappeared in 1981. Do you have news? Do you know where she is?"

The hope and fear warring in their eyes tore at me. I knew I had to tell them the whole truth. "I'm so sorry. I don't know anything about your daughter. Only her name and that she was married to Arthur Trent."

I told them about Maureen's disappearance, about Arthur's attempted suicide, the finding of the marriage certificate. As I talked I saw the hope fade from their eyes. When I finished, no one spoke for several minutes, then Mrs. Montgomery said, "Oh, poor Artie. Poor, poor Artie."

Her reaction surprised me. She must have read it on my face for she said, "He was such a nice boy, like a son to us. So quiet and serious. He truly loved Belinda. It nearly killed him when she ran away. She is our daughter and we loved her, still love her, but... well, she'd always been a little... not wild, exactly, just... flighty. We hoped so much that she would settle down. She did, too, after they were married but..." She shook her head. "Artie believed it was all his fault, that it was something he had said or done that had driven her away. Artie was a bright boy but he just never understood people." She grimaced. "I guess we never really understood Belinda, either. She was so beautiful. Honey, hand her that picture."

Curtis Montgomery silently handed me a photograph in a silver frame. I studied it. Belinda had indeed been a pretty girl but it was the laughter in her eyes, the sheer joy in her face that held you, that made you think she was more beautiful than she really was. There was capriciousness in the way she held her head and a recklessness in her smile that hinted at an unstable personality. A child/woman.

I handed the picture back. "You haven't heard from her since she disappeared?"

"Not a word." It was Curtis who answered, pain and anger

in his voice. "You'd think she could at least have let her mother know she was alive and safe, even if she didn't want us to find her."

"It just broke Artie's heart, the way she left. He quit his job, spent all of his savings trying to find her," she said.

"I hate to ask this but I have to know. Are they still married?"

"Oh, no. Artie divorced her. He didn't want to but after four years, we insisted. It wasn't fair to Artie. He was like a son to us, the son we never had. He needed to get on with his life."

"You're sure they were divorced?"

"Yes, of course. Artie left the papers with us when he moved to Seattle. In case Belinda came back."

"Could I have a copy of them?"

"Of course. Curt can make a copy tomorrow and bring it to you. Where are you staying?"

I gave them the name of the motel, listened to an hour of reminiscences, and finally got away. At least I would finally have some good news to report to my client. Arthur Trent wasn't a bigamist. Also, either Arthur Trent was one hell of an actor or he hadn't killed Belinda.

CHAPTER FIFTEEN

I drove back to the motel. Depression settled on me like a cold, wet blanket.

I'd felt lost and abandoned when my father died. While my mind understood that his abandonment hadn't been voluntary, emotionally I'd been devastated. For a long time, I'd hated him for leaving me. But I'd finally accepted my loss and adjusted. I'd had the comfort of visiting his grave.

The way Tony had deserted me had left indelible scars, but once I'd tracked him down, learned the truth, some of the pain and guilt had eased.

But these poor people had had no such comfort. There had been no closure for them. No answers, only questions.

It was a long time before I fell asleep.

I was barely dressed the next morning when Curtis Montgomery knocked on my door with photocopies of Arthur Trent's divorce papers. In the harsh morning light, his face was gray and haggard. The weariness in his eyes spoke clearly of a sleepless night.

"If you learn anything about our daughter, anything at all, will you let us know?"

I promised and watched him walk away, his shoulders hunched, his steps dragging. I realized he knew in his heart that his daughter was dead.

I'd been starving before Curtis had arrived but now I'd lost my appetite. I checked out and headed back to San Diego.

Judith R. Parker

It took me a while to find the San Diego Union offices but the girl in Archives was both pleasant and helpful. Looking at microfilm for any length of time always gives me a headache. Fortunately, it didn't take me long to find the story. It was toward the back of the paper, stuck between a piece on the delivery of a new fire truck to the town of Julian and an advertisement for cat food. The caption read: WOMAN BURNS TO DEATH IN EAST COUNTY CRASH.

It was a hurriedly written piece and the details were sketchy. It simply said:

Mary Whelan of Holtville died today when the car in which she was trapped exploded and burned after colliding with a second car. She was pronounced dead at the scene. Her husband, Henry Whelan, and the four unidentified occupants of the other car have been transported to San Diego hospitals. All are reported seriously injured. The California Highway Patrol and the San Diego Sherrif's Office are investigating the cause of the accident.

A witness arriving on the scene moments after the accident is quoted as saying, "It was horrible. Worse than any nightmare. That poor woman's screams. My husband tried to get to her but the heat and the flames were too intense. I saw her hair catch fire. It was terrible. Then the car just exploded."

I searched through another six months of issues but there was no further mention of the accident.

I wanted a cigarette. After thanking the clerk, I went outside and sat in my car. The picture created by the story was

143

very real in my mind. I could almost hear those screams. I couldn't imagine a more horrible way to die.

I finished my cigarette and lit another. Elliot Brill's father had either thrown around a small fortune in bribes or had one hell of a lot of political clout to have killed all but that one story.

I pulled out my map again. The caption had read "east county." I traced the Interstate from the Imperial County line to La Mesa. It was too far for a reporter from San Diego to have arrived in time to interview the passing motorist. A stringer must have called in the story. After almost twenty years, would the man still be around? The nearest town would have been Jacumba. The name rang a bell but for a moment I couldn't place it. Something to do with the movies. Then I had it. Rory Calhoun. A momentary wave of nostalgia filled me. I'd had a pre-adolescent crush on the handsome actor. He'd come from Jacumba. What had happened to him?

I crushed out the cigarette and went back inside. There was something else I wanted to check on. Dale Lockman was sure I was a reporter. That meant he had been involved in something newsworthy and I didn't think it was a twenty-year-old accident.

This time it took me a little longer to find what I was looking for. Two months previously, there had been a re-hash of an old murder case. I dug deeper and found the original story. In 1990, Dale Lockman had been arrested on suspicion of murdering his wife, Corinne Meecham Lockman. Her badly burned, partially decomposed body had been found on the beach off LaJolla in early April of that year. Cause of death had been a blow to the head and the body had been in the water at least a week, possibly longer. Charges had been filed in September of that year. The case had finally been dismissed for lack of evidence.

I followed the story through several weeks. The disappearance of Lockman's first wife was reiterated; several carefully worded questions about other unsolved murders were implied, barely escaping libel.

I went back to this year's story and read it again. No question that the story had been slanted against Dale Lockman, implying that only poor police procedures kept Lockman from paying for his crime. No wonder he had lost his temper when he thought I was a reporter. The press had had a field day with the poor unlucky guy.

I wanted to know more about the Whelan accident. Perhaps the reporter who had called in the original story could tell me. If I could find him. I located the Personnel Office. The gal was a snippy young thing who said the manager was on vacation and I couldn't see the assistant manager without an appointment. She probably hadn't even been born when Mrs. Whelan died, which made it ancient history to her, and she wasn't interested either in the story or in helping me.

In the lobby, I picked up a copy of that day's paper and riffled through it until I found a news story with a by-line. Crossing my fingers, I asked the receptionist if Jason Daniels was in and if I could see him. He was and I could.

I found the newsroom and Jason Daniels. He was in his mid-thirties and hadn't been with the paper long but said he'd ask around if I wanted to wait. I hung around, reading the paper for half an hour and finally left with a name. Russell (Rusty) Anders had been a stringer in the East County at one time but hadn't worked for the paper in years. He'd lived in Jacumba at the time, but the old-timer who'd known him didn't know if he was even alive.

I went back and sat in my car and smoked another

cigarette. I had the information I'd come to California for. The copies of the divorce papers were tucked in my briefcase. I should be on my way to the airport and a flight back to Seattle. But I wasn't going back, not yet. I jotted the time and the mileage in my notebook. From now on, I wasn't billing my client. This part was on me. It might be a wild goose chase but I had to know more about Henry Whelan.

As I drove east on Interstate-8, I couldn't put the thought of a serial killer out of my mind. On the other hand, it seemed much too far-fetched to be believable. I didn't *want* to believe it.

The accident that killed Mary Whelan had happened in 1976. Peggy Lockman had disappeared in 1979, Belinda/Buffy in 1981. According to Elliot Brill, his wife Marie had disappeared in March of 1985. I still didn't know if Abigail Steiner had disappeared but my gut told me I wouldn't find her happily going about her business. And Maureen had disappeared in March of this year. I started to eliminate Corinne, then changed my mind. She might have vanished, too, if her body hadn't washed ashore.

I pulled onto the shoulder, got out my notebook, and listed the missing women.

Peggy Lockman	*April*	*1979*
Belinda Trent	*?*	*1981*
Marie Brill	*March*	*1985*
Abigail Steiner	*?*	*?*
Corinne Lockman	*March*	*1990*
Maureen Trent	*March*	*199?*

Four out of five women had vanished. Five out of five if I counted Corinne. All had disappeared in the spring, three in

March. I flipped back through my notes, and despite the heat, broke out in a cold sweat. There was a definite pattern. Throwing the car in gear, I headed down the highway. I wanted to get to El Centro, find a motel, and call Sam.

An exit sign for Jacumba flashed in view and I slowed down. What the hell, I was here. It wouldn't hurt to check. Rusty Anders might still be around. From what Dainels had told me, he'd be an old man, but old people frequently liked to talk.

Jacumba turned out to be small, rundown and on the verge of becoming a ghost town. Even the park looked to be on its last legs, the grass patchy and dry, the trees drooping and dust covered. I drove a few blocks and was back in the high desert. If the town had always been depressed, I could understand why Rory Calhoun had left and headed for the big city and the silver screen. I would have wanted to escape, too.

Turning around, I drove back and parked across the street from the hotel. It had definitely seen better days. I was wondering if it was even open when a couple of old men came out, shuffled across the street and settled themselves on a rickety bench in the park. I got out and followed them.

It wasn't hard to start them talking. I learned that Jacumba, back in the horse and buggy days, had been a thriving resort due to its mineral baths. Also a place where many Imperial Valley residents had come to escape the summer heat. When I turned the talk to Rusty Anders, they both shook their heads. Neither remembered him.

I climbed back in my car and headed back to the freeway. I wasn't too disappointed. It had been a long shot, anyway.

The sun had disappeared behind the Lagunas when I pulled off the Freeway and checked into a Holiday Inn. I dumped my things on the bed and grabbed the telephone.

Missing!

There were a couple of calls I wanted to make before I talked to Sam.

Seth Steiner answered on the eleventh ring sounding either half asleep or half drunk. I didn't bother to introduce myself, just asked, "When did you last see Abigail?"

My shock tactics worked. He answered, "March 23, 1986." There was a pregnant pause, then he barked, "Who is this?"

I told him. If he'd been drinking, he sobered up fast. I listened to five minutes of angry sputterings that included phrases like *invasion of privacy, legal recourse, harassment,* and a few more obscenities than I would have expected from a college professor.

When he'd finally run out of breath and epithets, I told him I knew about the accident that had killed Mary Whelan. His bluster disappeared. "How did you find out? We agreed not to talk about it."

I told him how I found out didn't matter. "You never talked about your personal lives? Not in all these years?"

"No. We... we avoided each other after the accident. It seemed easier that way. You have to understand. It was an awful time for all of us. Dale was terribly mutilated; Artie had both legs broken so bad the doctors thought at first they would have to amputate; I had a skull fracture among other things. Elliot was the only one who didn't sustain major injuries, just a broken arm and some cuts and bruises."

"So you let Brill's father hush the whole thing up."

"Look, Miss Roarke, we were all just kids. My parents were alive but they were in Europe. Dale's folks were back east and there wasn't anything they could do anyway. They were piss poor. Artie didn't want his dad to know because he had a heart condition. Andrew Brill's attorneys came on like

148

gangbusters. Said they would take care of everything if we'd just sign a bunch of papers. We were in so much pain and so full of painkillers we didn't know which end was up.

"Hell, within twenty-four hours we were in this fancy private hospital in Napa County. Just before I was released from the hospital, they came around and explained what we'd signed. Then they showed me the hospital and doctors bills and said if I didn't abide by the agreement, I'd have to repay Mr. Brill." Steiner was blubbering by now. "We were just kids. You got to understand, we were just kids."

"You and Arthur Trent worked together for a couple of years. You never talked about it then?"

"No. We... well, we saw each other at work, but that's all. At first we tried to remain friends, but it just wasn't the same. We'd be out on a boat or at a picnic and one of us would remember...and...and in the end it was just easier not to see each other, socially. Then I quit and went back for my masters and we didn't see each other at all."

"You never had personal contact or visited in all these years?"

"No. I guess we were all too ashamed."

"But you did keep in touch."

"Yes, but only through the mail. Christmas cards, a postcard with a new address, that sort of thing. We... at least I, couldn't bear to lose contact completely. I guess the others felt the same way."

"Why did you get together at Brill's house last month?"

"That was my idea. Not a very good one, as it turned out. You probably won't understand, Miss Roarke, but for four years those three had been closer to me than my family. I loved them. After all this time, I thought we should be able to put what happened behind us. When the symposium was set up, I thought it would be a wonderful opportunity to... well, to renew old ties."

"Did it?"

"No. I don't think Elliot wanted us to stay with him but noblesse oblige and all that. I wrote to Artie and Dale asking them to come. Dale never bothered to answer, but Artie seemed as anxious as I was to mend things."

"And did you?"

"No. It was like meeting strangers. Only the faces were familiar. We sat around, being polite, talking about our work, the new boating safety laws, the EPA. Nice polite impersonal conversations. It wasn't a comfortable weekend."

"So you didn't discuss your personal life, your wives?"

"No."

"Will you tell me about your wife?"

"Why do you want to know?"

I told him then about the disappearances. When I finished, he didn't say anything for a several minutes but I could hear him breathing heavily. "I met Abigail shortly after I moved to the Los Angeles area. Her parents were both dead and she was living with an aunt in Pasadena. She was from England and hated California. I did, too, but I felt I needed some practical experience before I went back to school. I'd always planned a teaching career. The year after we were married I applied for graduate school. I knew she was unhappy, but... I came home from work one day and she was gone. The police found her car at the airport. I assumed she'd gone home to England, that she'd come back, when I moved here."

"You've never heard from her?"

"Not a word but I never gave up hope. You think–"

"I don't know. Perhaps she did go home. I'll let you know

if I learn more."

I hung up and filled in the date for Abigail Steiner on my notes. Then I called the Montgomerys and learned that Belinda had taken off on March 26th. I added that date to my list, then, after a moment, I scribbled Mary Whelan's name at the top.

I tried Sam at home but he didn't answer. I called the Seattle Police Department but they said he'd gone for the day. As a last resort, I called Mom.

The first thing she said was, "I wish you would come home," and the second thing was, "Are you sure you're getting enough to eat?"

"Mom, I'm fine. I should be through here in a couple of days."

She went into her usual harangue about my work, my lifestyle, and mostly my lack of a husband to take care of me.

I listened patiently until I could get a word in, then I asked, "Is Sam there?"

She suddenly got very defensive and I wondered if she was beginning to catch on to Sam's intent. I hoped so. Sam wasn't there. I finally got off the phone, kicked my shoes off, and leaned back on the bed.

I was having second thoughts about looking up Henry Whelan. If he had kidnapped and killed six women, he couldn't be sane. The thought of coming face to face with a serial killer scared the hell out of me.

I thought about going to the police but what could I tell them? All I had was a list of dates and suspicions. Besides, whom would I talk to? None of the disappearances had happened in Imperial County. Sam was the one I needed to talk to. He'd at least listen to me and he'd know whom to contact.

I got up, copied my list of names and dates, wrote a quick

note telling Sam my thoughts and suspicions, and stuck them in a hotel envelope. Tomorrow I'd find a post office and send it by overnight mail.

I decided there was no way I was going to face Henry Whelan, but since I was here, I would dig up whatever background information I could. Then I'd beat it back to Seattle and dump the whole thing in Sam's lap.

I thought of the gun locked away in my safe. It's not much of a gun, good for little except target practice, but I almost wished I had it with me.

CHAPTER SIXTEEN

The sky was a pale cerulean blue when I got up the next morning. By the time I'd had breakfast and found the post office, the temperature was already in the 80's. It was going to be a scorcher of a day.

There was no listing for Henry Whelan in the phone book, so after I mailed my notes to Sam, I found the courthouse and did a little research. Thank God the building was air-conditioned. A copy of the their marriage license showed Henry Whelan to have been twenty-six when he and Mary were married in 1960. That would have made him forty-two at the time of the accident and in his sixties now. Much older than I had supposed. Further investigation turned up property owned by the Whelans and I wrote down the address.

Leaving the courthouse was like walking into an oven. Not a cloud marred the brassy sky and no breath of breeze stirred the fronds of the tall palms. From habit, I'd locked the car and hadn't thought to roll down the windows. The air conditioner was still pouring out hot air by the time I drove a few blocks and found a Mexican restaurant. Sweat was streaming down my face and I was glad I wasn't wearing makeup. This time I left the car windows rolled down. If it was stolen, I'd let Budget worry about it.

Thankfully the restaurant was air-conditioned and even the clammy feel of my sweat-drenched clothes felt good. I ordered a combination plate and a beer. I don't really like beer but in this heat, the sweetness of a Coke would have left me even thirstier. The heat had given me a headache and I could have done without the piped Mexican music. I found a couple of aspirins in my purse and washed them down with the beer.

By the time the food arrived, my headache had begun to ease, and I was able to enjoy the meal. It was good but not as good as what Carmen makes at home. When the waiter took away my plate, I ordered another beer and gazed absently out the window. I dreaded going back into the heat. One thing for sure, I needed something cooler to wear.

I finished the beer, got back in the car, relieved that leaving the windows down had made the temperature inside at least bearable. Cruising down Main Street, I spotted a boutique. Fortunately I'm easy to fit and found a couple of cotton sundresses in my size. The saleswoman kindly snipped the tags from one of them and I left with my wool gabardine slacks and long sleeved blouse neatly folded in a bag.

It didn't take me long to find the Imperial Valley Press building and I spent the afternoon searching the back files for any mention of the Whelans. I found only two items of interest.

The first was a news story in 1969 about the death of Thomas Whelan, age 7, son of Mary and Henry Whelan. The boy had drowned in an irrigation canal. His obituary appeared in the next day's edition and I learned he was an only child. Only one other relative was mentioned, an uncle, Martin Korecky.

The brief news story about Mary Whelan's death was merely a recap of the story that had run in the San Diego Union. Her obituary was almost word for word as her son's. Three weeks later there was a short item about Henry Whelan being released from the hospital in San Diego and a longer article on the accident. The only new fact was that Mary had been four months pregnant at the time of her death.

Henry Whelan had not only lost his wife in the accident but also his unborn child. In none of the stories were the names of the boys in the other car mentioned.

Before I left the Press building, I found a telephone and looked up Martin Korecky. He was listed and I scribbled down his address. It was five o'clock so I joined the exodus of employees. I stood on the pavement trying to decide what my next move should be. Just thinking of coming face to face with Henry Whelan caused icy fingers to race down my spine and I shivered despite the heat.

I got in the car, and leaving all the windows open, turned the air conditioner on full blast, hoping the fan would blow out some of the heat that had built up. Within minutes, sweat was streaming down my face, my scalp was itching like crazy, and my dress was clinging to me like a wet bathing suit.

When the air coming from the vents finally began to cool, I raised the windows and backed out of the parking lot. According to the map I'd picked up earlier, Holtville was about ten miles east of El Centro. The road was a four lane divided highway, boasting nothing of interest except a rather attractive golf course with several dedicated foursomes. At least I assumed they were dedicated. In my opinion, anyone would have to be either dedicated or insane to play in this kind of heat.

The road narrowed to two lanes, made a sharp left turn over railroad tracks, then after a couple of blocks, turned right and I was in downtown Holtville. The town had obviously seen better days. I passed several empty and partially empty buildings then on my left was a pretty, tree shaded park. A tiny building on the southeast corner of the park proclaimed itself the Chamber of Commerce.

I turned the corner, parked in front of a hardware store, and crossed the street fully expecting the place to be closed. I was in luck. A tiny, gray-haired woman was coming around the counter carrying her purse as I opened the door.

"Oh, dear. I was just leaving," she said.

"I was just wondering if you had a city map."

The frown that had been forming was chased away by a smile. "Oh, is that all?" She picked up a brochure from the counter and handed it to me. "On the inside, dear."

I thanked her and backed out. She locked the door and hurried up the street, obviously anxious to get away before I could make any further requests.

The park was the coolest non-air-conditioned place I'd found all day. A light breeze had sprung up and lowered the heat to barely tolerable. I strolled across the grass and settled down on a bench to study the brochure. It proclaimed Holtville to be the Carrot Capitol of the World and that I was two months too late for the annual Carrot Festival. I opened it to the map and located the streets where Henry Whelan and Martin Korecky lived. From the size of the town, they wouldn't be hard to find.

Once I had my bearings, I refolded the brochure, tucked it in my purse, and walked around the stucco building that graced the center of the park and served as City Hall, police station, and fire hall.

The north side of the park was given over to a children's playground and picnic area. At one table, two old men were just settling down to play cribbage.

I walked back to my car and drove east. In less than two minutes, I was cruising by the house owned by Henry Whelan. It was an old house, rapidly falling into disrepair. The weeds and grass that choked the yard, almost obliterating the cracked walkway, were tall and dangerously dry. It had the abandoned look of a house long empty.

I drove on and located Martin Korecky's house. It was even older and smaller but was neatly painted, the lawn trimmed and watered. A rose garden graced one corner of the lawn and bougainvillea trailed in riotous purple profusion over a trellised porch.

I parked and walked up the neatly edged sidewalk, through a wire gate and between beds of nasturtiums and marigolds to the front door. The doorbell played *How Dry I Am.*

A Mexican woman, who came barely to my shoulder and was so wide she blocked the doorway, answered the door. "*El Senor no esta aqui.*"

Mr. Korecky wasn't home. I answered her in Spanish, asking when he would be home. She shrugged and started to close the door.

"Do you know where I can find him?" I asked.

She hesitated a moment, then said he was in the park playing cards, the same as every night. Remembering the two old men I had seen, I thanked her, got back in the car, and drove to the park.

The two men paid me no mind as I walked up so I watched them finish the game. The winner was a tall, spare old man with skin as brown and weathered as boot leather. His square, blunt face looked like it had been carved with a hatchet. His voice was surprisingly high as he said, "Skunked you again, Pete. You're beginning to smell worse than a polecat."

"Are you Martin Korecky?" I asked, moving closer to the table.

His eyes, pale blue but surprisingly bright, wandered over

me, lingered a moment on my breasts then traveled on to my face. "I am. Who might you be?"

"My name is Kerry Roarke. I wonder if I could speak to you for a moment?"

Pete had been eyeing me, too. Now he stood up, his brown eyes laughing as he looked from Korecky to me and back again. "Reckon I'll head on home. See you tomorrow." He looked back at me. "This old goat gives you a hard time, pretty lady, you just let me know and I'll whup him for you."

"Get on outta here, you dried up shrimp. Can't you see the lady wants to talk to me."

Chuckling, Pete hobbled away. I watched him for a minute, then sat down in the spot he had vacated. Korecky was shuffling the cards and I watched the long, calloused fingers as he dexterously dealt out two hands. "You play cribbage?" he asked. There was something about the way he used his hands that reminded me of Andy McManus, my flute playing eye surgeon friend. They were competent hands.

I nodded and moved the pegs on the board to starting position. "I'd like to ask you some questions."

He motioned to the cards in front of me. "We'll play a game first. You any good?"

I shrugged. "It's been a long time since I've played."

"It'll come back to you."

It did, but I soon realized I was way out of my league. By the end of six hands, he was over thirty pegs ahead of me. I decided I needed to distract him. "I understand you're Henry Whelan's brother-in-law."

His fingers hesitated only a fraction of a second in the deal. "That's right. He was married to my sister, Mary."

"The Mary Whelan that was killed in an auto accident in 1976?"

158

"That's right."

I cut the deck, glanced at my cards, and threw down a card. "Seven."

He chuckled, slapped down an eight. "Fifteen for two." He pegged the two while I glowered.

I hadn't made a dent in his concentration. Something more drastic was needed. "Is Henry in town now?" I asked, laying down a queen. "Twenty-five."

He laid down a six. "Thirty-one for two. No, Henry hasn't been around for quite a while." He gave me a sharp look from under bushy eyebrows. "You want to know about Henry?"

"Yes."

"Okay. After we finish this game. Now you concentrate."

We finished the game in silence. He didn't quite skunk me. I managed to get three pegs over the skunk line before he pegged out. He put the cards and pegs away and stood. "Let's go to the house. Maria will have dinner waiting."

"Mr. Korecky, perhaps it would be better if we talked here. Some of the things I have to ask may be upsetting, unpleasant."

He looked me right in the eye and said, "That don't surprise me none. You walkin' or drivin'?"

"Driving."

"Good. I'll ride with you. After dinner I'll answer any of your questions I've a mind to. Fair enough?"

He headed straight for the Lincoln so I knew he'd seen me drive up. There was one question I had to ask before I got in the car. "Is Henry Whelan at your house or likely to come by?"

He had the passenger door half open. He stopped and gave me a long, searching look before sliding into the car. "Nope, Henry ain't been around these parts for some time, and if'n he was, he wouldn't come around. Now, let's go eat. I don't remember too good on an empty stomach."

There was no sign of Maria when we got to the house, but the air was redolent of her efforts in the kitchen. The inside of the house was as neat and well kept as the outside. We passed through a small living room, the furniture old and eclectic but solid, obviously purchased for comfort rather than style. What had originally been the dining room had been turned into a den, furnished with a worn recliner facing a television set in one corner. Built-in bookshelves covered three walls, filled to overflowing with books, mostly paperbacks. In the center was a long table, covered with sketches and drawings, tissue paper and balsa wood. The faint odor of Testor's Cement mingled with scent of cooking. From the ceiling hung a dozen or more model airplanes.

The room intrigued me. I'd have loved to browse through the books and study the models. I didn't get a chance for more than a quick look as Martin shepherded me on into the kitchen.

It was a cheerful room, painted a bright yellow with gleaming white appliances and cabinets on two walls. A round oak table and two captains chairs with yellow print cushions sat in a bow window with ruffled white curtains. A single place had been set at the table.

Martin gestured toward the second chair. "Have a seat."

I settled into the chair and studied what I could see of the back yard while Martin collected a second place setting and carried the food to the table. In the gathering dusk, there wasn't much to see but I could make out a large garden plot between the house and the alley. A blue pickup was parked in a gravel parking area.

He removed the cover from a clay pot and the sight and scent of homemade tamales sent my salivary glands working overtime. Frijoles refritos bubbled in a second pot. He sat down and unwrapped a stack of steaming flour tortillas.

He must have read my expression, for he chuckled and said, "Well, dig in."

I didn't argue. Food is one of my greatest weaknesses and this smelled heavenly. We were both concentrating too much on the food to bother with talk. Martin's Maria was every bit as good a cook as my Carmen.

Finally sated, I leaned back. Martin was watching me with a satisfied smile on his face. Without a word, he collected the dishes and stacked them in the sink, returning with an oversized ashtray.

"Hope you don't mind, but I like a smoke after dinner."

"I don't mind, if you don't," I said, rifling through my purse for my pack of Camel Lights.

He pulled a can of tobacco and book of papers out of his pocket and I watched with fascination as he rolled a cigarette. I'd read descriptions of the act in western novels, but this was the first time I'd actually seen it done.

When we'd both lit up, he leaned back, looked me straight in the eye, and asked, "Okay, Miss Roarke, what has that crazy bastard done now?"

CHAPTER SEVENTEEN

I hesitated, then asked, "Why do you think he's done something?"

"Look, Miss Roarke, when a pretty little lady like you comes around asking questions, I know something's going on. Are you one of those Mental Health people?"

The question shocked me. "Mental Health? No. Why would they be asking about Henry?"

"'Cause the poor fool ain't been right in the head since his boy died. He's been in and out of mental hospitals half a dozen times in the last twenty years." He stubbed out his cigarette and began rolling another one. "If you ain't from Mental Health, who are you?"

I got out a card and slid it across the table. "I'm a private detective from Seattle. Do you know where Henry is now?"

He fingered the card then laid it back on the table. "Last I heard he was up your way. Want to tell me what this is about?"

"I'll be honest with you, Mr. Korecky, I'm here on a wild guess. Before I say anything, would you tell me all you know about Henry?"

He lit the cigarette and stared at me through the smoke. "That could take some doing. I've known Henry Whelan for over forty years. What exactly do you want to know?"

"Everything you can tell me."

"Let me start some coffee, then. It's going to be a long

night."

When he had the Mr. Coffee going, he sat back down and leaned his elbows on the table. "Well, now, let's see, I first met Henry back in the late fifties. He was stationed out at the Naval Air Station. He was from somewhere's back east, West Virginia, Tennessee, one of them mountain states. Ain't rightly sure which one."

He shifted to stare out the window. "We'd never been what you'd really call religious but after mother died, Mary started going to one of those fundamentalist churches over in El Centro. Or was it Imperial? Brawley? I don't remember. Anyway, that's where she met Henry. They went together until he was transferred, then they wrote each other for about a year. When he got his discharge, Henry came back, got a job at the old onion dehydrating plant and they were married. I never cared much for Henry, but, well, Mary and I never had been all that close. She was some younger'n me. 'Sides, it was her life. Didn't figure I had any right to interfere."

He looked back at me. "Things was okay, normal, I mean, 'cepting they took their religion a bit too serious fer my taste, if you know what I mean."

He shrugged, glancing at me out of the corner of his eye. "I ain't got nothing against religion, don't get me wrong. I just ain't much on prayin' and fastin' and carryin' on. Like I say, things weren't too bad until the boy died. Mary took it real hard but nothing like Henry did. Claimed God took Tommy as a punishment for their sinning."

He stared at me defiantly. "Mary was no sinner! As sweet a woman as you'll ever meet. Until that bastard went to work on her. He was a self-righteous prig and he turned her into one."

The fire died out of his eyes. "Is that what you wanted to

know?"

"What about after Mary died?"

"Now that's something that's always puzzled me. Knowing Henry, I'd've expected him to make a big stink. From what he let drop when he first got out of the hospital, the kids in the other car were all dead drunk. Henry called any form of alcohol "the devil's brew." Hell, if he'd lived back then, he'd've been swinging an ax right along with Carrie Nation. But he never said a word after that first night. Not a word."

"Could he have been bought off?"

"Henry? You mean paid to keep his mouth shut? Hell, no."

He got up and poured us each a cup of coffee, nudging a pitcher of cream and sugar bowl toward me. I stirred some of both into the cup and asked, "Are you sure?"

"You've got something in mind. Better tell me."

So I told him about Brill's father paying off the three boys, about the lack of coverage by the news media. "Brill was obviously able to smooth over the whole incident. Even with all his money and pull, I don't think he could have swung it if Henry Whelan had pursued the matter."

Martin stirred his coffee absently and it was a long time before he finally spoke. "A month or so after he came home from the hospital, Henry quit his job. To my knowledge, he ain't worked a day since. I always figured he must have got a pretty good settlement from the insurance company and Henry never was one to live high on the hog."

"Has he been here all the time since the accident?"

"No. In fact he only comes back for a few months every couple of years."

"Do you know where he goes or what he does when he's away?"

He shook his head. "I don't see much of him. Sometimes the only way I know he's back is when I drive by his house and see the yard's been mowed. About the only time I hear from him is when he sends me a picture postcard. Once in a while, he'll give me a call while he's home. He's crazy as a loon and gettin' crazier. Says he's been doing the Lord's work. He always was one for spouting the bible, but the last time he was home he couldn't even do that right. Yelling about the sin of wages and a wife for a wife and vengeance granted by the Lord. Hell, I ain't no bible reader but even I know it's "an eye for an eye' and 'vengeance is mine, sayeth the Lord'."

He took a sip of coffee, and grinned. "I reckon he was hidin' behind the outhouse when the Lord was givin' out brains, and now he's lost what few he had."

It took a minute for his words to register and then I wasn't sure I'd heard right. "What did you say?" The words came out in a squeak.

"Huh?"

"Wife. You said he said wife." I wasn't making sense and I knew it.

Martin was staring at me over the rim of his cup. Slowly he lowered the cup and set in carefully in the saucer. "He said something about a wife for a wife."

CHAPTER EIGHTEEN

My heart dived into my stomach then lurched back into place, slamming against my ribs like a caged beast. The coffee cup slipped through my fingers, shattering both cup and saucer and sending a shower of hot coffee onto the table.

Martin leaped up, grabbed a dishtowel, and tried to stop it from flowing into my lap. He looked at my face, dropped the towel, and pulled my chair back. The room was spinning crazily. I felt his hand on my neck forcing me forward. From a distance I heard his voice saying, "Put your head between your knees. Breath deep. That's it. Nice and slow. Deep. Breathe deep."

I could feel the blood rushing back to my face and the room stopped spinning. "I'm okay," I whispered.

He let go of my neck and I sat up, thoroughly embarrassed. *I don't faint, damn it. Never!* I looked up and tried to smile but my lips felt like two slabs of Parawax. Martin was looking at me, his face furrowed with anxiety. "Are you sure you're okay? How about a glass of water?"

I nodded. My mouth was as dry as the desert outside. "Please." The word came out in a hoarse croak.

He brought me the water and I gulped it down. Handing the glass back I started to apologize but he cut me off. "Never mind that. What did I say that made you turn white as a sheet?"

I waved away the question. "Do you know where Henry

was during any of the times he was away?"

"Sometimes," he admitted.

"How?"

"He sent me postcards."

"Do you still have them?"

"I have the first one he sent and maybe a couple of others. Why?"

"May I see them?"

"I reckon, but there's nothing on them but bible verses, mostly misquoted."

I stood up and laid a hand on his arm. "Please, they could be very important."

He looked at me for a moment and I could tell he was wondering if I was crazy, too. Finally, he put a hand under my elbow. "Come on. They're in the other room."

He guided me back to the den and seated me in the recliner. I had the chance to survey the room but I was no longer interested. From one of the bookcases, he took a couple of deed boxes. He moved a stack of paperback books from the side table, put the boxes down and turned on the lamp and settled himself on the floor beside my chair. Wordlessly, he opened the first one and began sorting through the letters inside.

I wanted a cigarette badly but my purse was in the other room. I saw a Marlboro box on top of the television and asked for one. He looked up, and for the first time since I'd started my questioning, he laughed. Clutching the deed box to his chest, he reached up and handed me the pack and a book of matches. I flipped the top and saw why he'd laughed. The box was full of hand rolled cigarettes. He watched me light one, then went back to his sorting.

The acrid smoke burned my throat and I choked. Ignoring

his chuckle, I took another drag. It was still strong but the smoke went down smoothly this time. The nicotine rush made me dizzy for a moment but I liked the taste.

He grunted and I dropped the cigarette in the ashtray. "You've found something? Let me see."

He handed me the post card. I took it gingerly, holding it by the edges. There probably wouldn't be any usable prints after all this time, but I wasn't taking any chances. It was a view of the Golden Gate Bridge. I turned it over. It was postmarked September 20, 1978.

The handwriting was small and cramped. It read:

I have seen the wicked in great power and spreading himself.

My hand was trembling as laid the card on the table. "Are there more?"

A few minutes later he handed me a second card. It, too, was from San Francisco, a picture of Coit Tower, dated April 2, 1979.

The same cramped hand had written:

I have punished the wicked for their iniquities.

Martin had put that box aside and was riffling through the second one. "You can see how crazy he is. That isn't even a correct quote."

"Maybe not, but–"

"Here," he said, handing me two more cards. My skin was crawling as I took the cards. The first was a picture of the Queen Mary and was stamped Long Beach, April 9, 1986.

It read: *The wicked cease from troubling*

The last card was of the Space Needle, dated March 20th, the day after Maureen disappeared. This time the writing was even less legible, as if written under great stress.

The wicked flee.

Under the quote, in larger letters, heavily underscored was written: *BUT THE LORD SHALL NOT BE DENIED.*

I looked up and found Martin watching me intently. I had to swallow the bile that was burning the back of my throat before I could speak. "Are there any more?"

He shook his head. "I must have thrown the rest out."

"But there were more? Do you remember where they came from or when?"

He put the box aside and lit a cigarette. "I got one a couple of years ago from San Diego. The same kind of biblical quote. I can't tell you much about the others, except they were always a year or more apart and I think they were all mailed from various places in California. Except that last one. You want to tell me what's going on?"

"I can only tell you what I know and the conclusions I've drawn. And I'll only tell you if I may have these cards."

He hesitated, searching my face, then he sighed and nodded. "I reckon you can have them. Now tell me what Henry's done."

"First, do you have a plastic bag?" He started for the kitchen and I said, "Would you bring my purse?"

He came back with a plastic bag and my purse. I slipped cards inside the bag and rummaged through my purse for my notebook. I tore a sheet from my notebook and handed it to him. "Would you mind writing a note to the effect that you are giving me these cards of your own free will. Oh, and please date and sign it."

I wanted the note for two reasons; in case he should later claim I'd stolen them, and also, in the event there were any fingerprints, I wanted to be able to eliminate his. When he finished the note, I had him slide it inside the bag and sealed it.

"Now, what's going on?" he asked.

"This could take awhile," I said, picking up the plastic bag and purse and standing. "How about another cup of coffee?"

We went back to the kitchen. While Martin poured the coffee, I tucked the cards away in my purse and lit a Camel. After Martin's home-rolled cigarette, it didn't have much flavor.

"Does Henry know the names of the boys?"

"In the car that killed Mary? This has something to do with that accident? It was nearly twenty years ago."

"Does he know the names?" I repeated.

"Well, now, I reckon as how he does, one or two, anyway. When I visited him in the hospital, he was ranting about the driver. Called him by name. Never mentioned it after he came home, though, but that don't mean nuthin' 'cause we never did talk about the accident."

I told him about the disappearance of Maureen Trent and what I had learned during my investigation. When I finished, Martin sat with his head bent, his fingers toying with the handle of his cup. Without looking up, he finally said, "You think Henry harmed all them women?"

"I don't *know*, but, yes, I *think* he did."

"You figure on going to the police?"

I couldn't lie. "Yes."

He looked up then. "I can't say I ever thought much of Henry. He's always been a mite too opinionated in his beliefs for my taste, but I never thought he could do anything like..." He sighed. "If Henry killed all them women, then I reckon he's got to be stopped."

"Do you have a recent picture of Henry?" I asked.

"Not recent, no." He left the room and came back a few minutes later with a couple of snapshots. One was of a couple I assumed to be Mary and Henry, and judging from their

170

clothes and their age, had been taken not long before the accident. The other was of Henry alone, taken about the same time. He was of about average height, skinny, his hair already thinning. His face was nondescript, except for the pinched mouth and the burning eyes.

They were black and white photos, so I asked, "What color is his hair? His eyes?"

"His hair used to be brown but he ain't got much left. His eyes are sorta gray, real light."

I handed back the picture with Mary, retaining the picture of Henry alone. "May I keep this one?"

He nodded and I tucked it in my purse with the postcards.

"What you going to do now?" he asked.

I knew what had to be done and the thought scared me silly. "I want to see the inside of Henry's house."

He stared at me for a long time, then nodded. "I'll get the key."

"You have a key?"

"If Henry ain't changed the locks since Mary died, I do."

He disappeared into the den, returning a few minutes later with a ring of keys. "Reckon we'd best take my truck."

I followed him out the back door and across the yard. He opened the door for me, a courtesy I wasn't used to but decided I liked.

A few minutes later he pulled up in front of the Whelan house. I was relieved to see that it was still dark.

Martin climbed out, saying, "You wait here. I'll make sure Henry hasn't come back."

The sun had dropped behind the mountains and the air had cooled, but I was wet with nervous perspiration. My nerves were vibrating like plucked guitar strings by the time Martin returned.

"He ain't here. Let's go."

I followed him up the cracked walk and into the house. Martin turned on the light and I glanced quickly around the room. It was obvious that no one had been here in some time. Every surface was covered with dust and cobwebs decorated the corners. I wanted to see the rest of the house and Martin went ahead of me turning on lights.

The front bedroom was obviously the one Henry and Mary had shared. The double bed was unmade, as if someone had just risen, but the exposed sheets were covered with dust. I pulled open the drawers of the single dresser and got a shock. Three of the drawers still contained a woman's wear. I stepped back as Martin reached out to stroke a pink, moth-eaten sweater.

He answered my unasked question. "Mary's. I gave her that sweater on her last birthday." He withdrew his hand and went into the hall.

I did a quick search but found nothing of interest. I didn't bother with the bathroom or the tiny back bedroom that still contained the clothes and toys of a seven-year-old boy.

For a moment I felt a twinge of sympathy for Henry Whelan, but only for a moment.

In the kitchen, I struck pay dirt. One whole wall was taken up with white painted cabinets. On the bottom shelf of the first top cabinet was a stack of newspapers. I pulled out the top one, shook the dust off, and read the masthead. It was a San Diego Union. I riffled through the stack. They were all the Union, from 1980 through 1993.

I glanced at Martin and opened the rest of the doors. Each cabinet was filled with newspapers, separate stacks for Los Angeles, San Francisco, Boston, and Seattle. At least ten years of each. The bottom cabinets contained stacks of boating magazines.

I pulled open the drawers that ran down the center of the cabinets. The first four contained only cooking utensils and the usual junk that clutters such drawers, but the last was filled with newspaper and magazine clippings. On the top, held together with a paper clip were articles from several papers and magazines about the symposium in San Francisco.

Martin pulled out the drawer and carried it to the kitchen table. Using a dishtowel, he dusted off two of the chairs and I went to work. Half an hour later, any doubts I might have had, had disappeared.

Henry Whelan had not only known all four of the boy's names, but he had kept close track of them over the years. Every newsworthy event had been collected, including wedding announcements. On the top of one stack, Maureen's face stared up at me from the grainy newspaper.

I returned the clippings to the drawer and Martin replaced it in the cabinet. I thought about taking them, but didn't want to risk them being thrown out as tainted evidence. It didn't matter that Martin had let me in with a key; I still had no legal right to be in this house.

We rode back to Martin's place in silence. He walked me through the yard to my car. "What are you going to do now?" he asked, as I slid behind the wheel.

"Fly back to Seattle in the morning."

Laying a hand on my shoulder, he looked down at me. "You be careful. If he's really killed all them women, well, you just be careful."

I drove back to the motel, called Alaska Airlines and booked a flight from San Diego to Seattle for midmorning, then left an early wake-up call with the desk. I took a shower to get rid the sweat that was beginning to itch, then added a full report on what Martin Korecky had told me to my notes. I went to bed but didn't get much sleep. Too many nightmares. I now knew there was a definite connection between Maureen and Henry Whelan.

I skipped breakfast and was on the road before daylight the next morning. I turned in my car at the Budget counter and got stuck with a drop-off charge. On the flight, I studied the photograph of Henry Whelan. Something was nagging at the back of my mind but I couldn't get it into focus.

After the heat of the desert, it was a relief to walk out into the cool Seattle rain. Even the exhaust fumes from the cruising cars and busses smelled different, cleaner.

I claimed my car and drove straight to my office, parked and walked up the street. I stopped on the pavement sucking in the moist air, tasting the salty tang, relishing the scent of the sea, glad to be back in God's Country.

Inside, I ignored the flashing red light on the answering machine and called Sam, only to learn that he was taking a late lunch. I left a message for him to return my call and tried Mary Sue but got her machine. I left a message that I needed a report typed right away.

Uncovering my typewriter, I went to work transcribing my notes. I'm the world's worst typist and when I finished, the pages were full of correction fluid and typos but I knew Sam wouldn't care.

I keep boxes of Ziploc bags in my office to use as evidence bags. I emptied the postcards onto my desk, then carefully slid each one into a separate bag. I knew Sam would want the originals but I wanted photocopies for my records. When I first opened my office, I had to take everything to a copy shop down the street and it became such a drag, I'd bought a good machine of my own. It hadn't by any means paid for itself yet, but it was worth the investment for the convenience. I'd just finished making photocopies of the postcards and the notes I'd typed when Sam returned my call. I asked, "Did you get my notes?"

"Hell, yes. Did all that smog in California scramble your brains or are you pulling my leg?"

"Sam, I'm dead serious and that's no pun. Can you come over? I've got something more I think you should see."

"Kid, you're way out in left field. Trent killed his wife. He as good as confessed."

"Sam, just come over. I've got a lot more to tell you, but I don't want to go into it on the phone."

He didn't answer for several seconds while I waited impatiently. Finally he said, "You're serious about this?"

"Damned right I am."

"Okay, I've got some things to clear up here but I'll be over in about an hour."

I hung up and played back the messages on the answering machine. One call was a computerized sales call and I fast-forwarded after the first few words. Whatever they were selling, I didn't want any. The second was also a sales pitch, but at least the voice was human, so I did him the courtesy of listening to his spiel, even though I wasn't interested in vinyl siding. The third call was from a corporate client wanting me to check out a new employee. I called him back and he agreed they could wait a few days, and in the meantime, they'd send me over a copy of the guy's resume and application. The last call was from Angela Bottoms of Clean Sweep. She was going out of town for a few days but wondered if she could see me when she got back. She added that it had nothing to do with Maureen Trent.

One hour became two and then three and still Sam didn't

show. I was ready to start pacing the floor when he finally opened the door. I barely gave him a chance to sit down before handing him the report I'd typed. "Don't say anything, just read this, then I'll answer your questions."

A couple of times he sent me sharp glances over the top of the pages, *humpffed* a time or two, but made no comment until he reached the end of the last page. Then, aligning the papers on the edge of my desk, he said, "You have the original postcards?"

"Yes." I took them out of a drawer and handed them to him. I also handed him the picture of Henry Whelan. "Any chance your department could computer age this photograph?"

"Nah, but I can see what our sketch artist can come up with. Now tell me about the Montgomerys. Not just the conversation. I want you to describe their reactions, their body language, your impressions, everything."

When I'd finished relating my interviews with Buffy's parents, he had me start at the beginning, my first meeting with Ian Donlevy and took me through the whole case. I had to go over the conversations with Lockman and Korecky so many times, my voice was beginning to crack. I could tell he wasn't happy about my visit to the Whelan house but he let it pass with only a brief glare. He put me through an interrogation that left me feeling thankful that I was a friend and not a suspect.

I was utterly exhausted by the time he finally said, "They've closed the case."

"What! Why?"

"Didn't I tell you? Arthur Trent died this morning. That's why I was so late getting here."

CHAPTER NINETEEN

I don't know why Arthur Trent's death hit me so hard. I'd never even met the man but tears were building behind my eyelids. Perhaps it was because I'd been thinking about my father a lot lately, missing him more than I had in years.

Anger and resentment grabbed me, drying the tears before they could fall. It wasn't fair that he should die without at least knowing the truth. I needed to channel my anger. I glared at Sam. "Shit! Did he regain consciousness? Give you a statement?"

"No."

I narrowed my eyes, still glaring. "I suppose you think that closes the case. Well, you're wrong!" I was so angry I couldn't sit still. I jumped up and began to pace. "You don't even know Maureen Trent is dead, for God's sake!"

"She's dead, all right. The body will turn up eventually."

I stopped pacing, and leaning my hands on the windowsill, stared down at the street, watching two homeless men arguing without really seeing them. "I'm not so sure she is dead."

"Come on, Kerry. Trent as good as confessed."

I rested my forehead against the cool glass. In a way, I could understand Sam's attitude. Arthur Trent's death had provided them with a nice, neat solution and they could get on with solving the myriad crimes that threaten to inundate any big city police department. I was tempted to back off, let it go, but the thought of all those other women stopped me.

"Sam, if he meant that message to be a confession, why didn't he say so? It doesn't make sense."

"It makes as much sense as your idea that this Whelan killed her in revenge for the twenty year old death of his wife."

Sam came around the desk and put a hand on my shoulder. "Come on, kid, you're letting this case get under your skin. You're reaching and you know it. Let it go."

I shrugged off his hand. "No. One way or another, dead or alive, I'll find Maureen. That's what I was hired to do."

I turned to face him. "Did you read that last postcard, the one mailed from here? 'The wicked flee.' It is postmarked the day after she disappeared. I think she was still alive when that was sent. I think Whelan spooked her and she's hiding. I think he's still here, still hunting for her."

"Kerry—"

"Damn it, Sam, it's possible." I sat down and pulled out the copy of the card and handed it to him. "Forget Arthur Trent for a minute. Read that again, with an open mind."

He glanced at it, tossed it back on the desk, and picked up my report and the plastic bags. "This isn't enough to reopen the case."

"Sam—"

"It isn't. But I will see what we can do with the photograph and I'll request copies of the police reports on these other women. That's all I can do."

"At least see what the lab can come up with in the way of fingerprints. There should be a good set of Martin Korecky's prints on the note I had him write."

His hand was on the knob when I thought of something else. "Sam, run a check on Henry Whelan. See if he has any kind of record." I was remembering Martin Korecky asking if I was a Mental Health worker and his idea that Whelan had been in and out of mental hospitals. "Find out if he has ever been committed for psychiatric evaluation and the dates."

"Kerry, for Pete's sake–"

"Please, humor me in this." I looked him square in the eye. "And, Sam, if Henry Whelan is a serial killer, what could happen if Dr. Steiner or Elliot Brill or Dale Lockman marry again?"

He stared at me for a moment through narrowed eyes, then he was gone.

I considered calling Ian Donlevy but decided it could wait until morning. I was utterly exhausted and wanted nothing so much as food, followed by a long hot soak in the Jacuzzi and my own bed. I called Carmen to let her know I'd be home soon, locked the office, and headed for my car.

Clouds, black with rain, were brushing the tops of the tall buildings as I walked up the street. They looked as heavy and depressed as I felt. Homeless men wrapped in ragged blankets and plastic bags, like so many bundles of trash, huddled in doorways. The rain came as I crossed the parking lot, drenching me before I could unlock the car and dive inside.

The weather suited my mood. The windshield wipers could barely keep up with the torrent and wind gusts buffeted the car. It was as if the heavens were as angry and resentful as I was.

Lights were burning in all the downstairs rooms when I got home. I dashed for the kitchen door carrying only my briefcase, knowing Julio would unload my luggage in the morning. The heady aroma of fresh baked bread as I opened the door made my stomach growl. The dogs met me, prancing and whining. Even Nefertiti came to greet me, although more slowly and with true cat dignity. A glance around the kitchen told me Carmen had gone home. I was glad, because much as I like and appreciate her, I was in no mood for her questions.

My depression began to lift. It was good to be home. "Down, guys. Let me get out of these wet clothes and I'll pet you."

I dropped my suitcase in the den and went upstairs, Nefertiti dashing ahead, the dogs at my heels. Carmen must have read my mind for the Jacuzzi was bubbling. I stripped, and not bothering with a shower, slipped into the hot water, inching down until it reached my chin. With a sigh of pure contentment, I closed my eyes and let the water work its magic.

As the chill finally left my bones and my muscles relaxed, I began to talk to the dogs, telling them about the case. Shybaby whined, and laying her jaw on the edge of the Jacuzzi, gazed at me in commiseration. Wiley sat, head cocked expectantly. Dogs make great confidants. They never, well, almost never, interrupt. They never argue or reveal a confidence and always believe everything I say. That's a lot more than I can say about a lot of people.

Warm and relaxed, I went downstairs, satisfied my hunger with a bowl of beef stew eaten with hunks of fresh homemade bread dripping with butter. I was in no mood to worry about my cholesterol level. I thought about getting out my notes and going over them but I was simply too tired and depressed. Tomorrow would be soon enough.

The dogs followed me through the house as I checked the locks, turned off lights, and went upstairs. They seemed to know I needed company. With Nefertiti purring on the pillow beside me and one dog on the floor on each side of the bed, I went to sleep.

The smell of brewing coffee woke me the next morning. I got up and headed for the bathroom, noticing that Carmen had been in. My suitcase was open on a chair, waiting to be unpacked, and my wet clothes had been taken away. Rain still pattered on the roof, telling me the weather hadn't improved.

I showered, dressed in a wool suit, and hurried downstairs. Carmen greeted me with a smile, a fresh squeezed glass of orange juice, and a stack of mail and messages. I glanced through them as I sipped the juice. I was only half way through the mail when she slid a plate of chorizo and scrambled eggs in front of me.

"Your mama call. She wants you to come to dinner Sunday night."

"I'll give her a call."

"She already gone. Say she won't be back until late."

I nodded and went back to the mail, sorting out the bills, throwing away the advertisements and circulars that made up the bulk of it. Carrying the bills, I went to the den. None were pressing and I tossed them aside to pay later.

I called my client. Ian sounded as depressed as I'd felt the night before. I brought him up to date on everything I'd learned.

"You think this Henry Whelan killed Maureen?"

"I think Whelan is a more likely suspect that Arthur Trent."

He didn't say anything for a moment, so I went on, "There are a few things that don't quite fit. Things I'd like to check into. Did you get the financial information I asked for?"

"How did you know Maureen had transferred money?"

"I didn't. It was just a hunch. How much did she transfer and where?"

"That's what I don't understand. She had a savings account with over two hundred thousand dollars and over thirty thousand in a checking account. She closed both and had the money transferred to an account in the Cayman Islands. She took all but five thousand out of their joint savings."

"How much did she take?"

"Eighteen thousand."

"How did she take it and when?"

"A cashier's check, on the day before she disappeared. The same day, she wrote a check for cash for three thousand on their joint checking account.

"What was she going to do with all that money? And where did she get it? I don't understand any of this."

I thought I did but I wasn't ready to tell Ian. He obviously loved his sister, and if what I suspected was true, it would break his heart. I decided to change the subject.

"Did either Maureen or Arthur leave a will?"

"God, I don't know. To tell the truth I hadn't thought about it."

"Did your sister have a regular doctor?"

"Doctor?" He repeated the word as if he'd never heard it before.

"Yes. Any particular doctor she went to on a regular basis, a family doctor?"

"Only Dr. Magnuson."

"Do you know him?"

"Sure. He's been the family doctor since before my parents died. Why?"

"I'd like to ask him some questions about your sister. Would you mind giving him a call and asking him to see me? Tell him you'd appreciate his cooperation. Can you do that?"

He agreed and gave me Dr. Magnuson's office address. Then he told me the time and place of Arthur Trent's funeral services on Saturday and asked me if I would come. The request was almost a plea and I couldn't ignore it. Although I hate funerals, I said I would be there. I felt I owed it to him. I sure hadn't made any progress in finding his sister.

I debated mentioning the possibility that Maureen might be in hiding but decided not to get his hopes up. Despite what I'd told Sam, I didn't really believe it myself. Still, it was a possibility, but one I'd keep to myself a while longer.

After he hung up, I pulled out the case file and went over all of my notes. Then something that had been nagging at the back of my mind for days finally clicked as I re-read my notes on the visit to the cleaners. The girl had said a man had accosted Maureen as she went back to the car. I read the description again. *A white man, short and skinny, wearing baggy pants, looking like a bum.* I flipped through my notes until I found Claudia Oliver's statement. *A homeless man had followed Maureen up the street.*

Henry Whelan.

I was sure of it. Henry Whelan *had* been stalking Maureen. Had he caught up with her or had she indeed become spooked and run away? I copied out that portion of my notes and stuffed them in my purse. Putting everything else back in my briefcase, I grabbed a raincoat and took off.

It was raining heavily as I drove through the foothills but had eased to a drizzle by the time I crossed the I-90 floating bridge. A traffic accident held me up and it was almost noon when I got downtown but Sam was in.

He peered up at me from under shaggy brows, and before I could speak, he said, "Wait. You can tell me over lunch."

He took me to the India Taj in Pioneer Square. The place was practically empty. We took a table in the back, the smoking section. As soon as we placed our orders, he said, "Okay, let's have it."

I shoved the copies I'd made of the two conversations across the table. He read them and tossed them back. "Kerry, that doesn't mean a thing. Do you know how many guys these descriptions would fit?"

"It would also fit Henry Whelan. He was stalking her, Sam. I know he was."

"Prove it."

"Get me that composite picture and I will."

"You aren't going to give up, are you?"

"If I'm right, he's already killed five women. Six, if he's found Maureen. Hell, no, I'm not going to give up."

The waiter, wearing a green turban and full beard, brought our tandoori chicken and we didn't speak again until we'd finished eating. Sam insisted on getting the check, and as we walked out, he asked, "You going back to your office?"

"Yes."

"I'll have the picture for you this afternoon."

My corporate client had sent the application and resume on their new employee. I made a few calls, starting the ball rolling. I do a lot of these kinds of background checks and have it down to a science. With all of the relocating people do nowadays, I've established working relations with a number of agencies scattered around the country. It's easier, cheaper and generally provides better information to sub out the out-of-town inquires.

Figuring Ian had had enough time to contact Dr. Magnuson, I looked up the phone number and gave him a call. His receptionist told me the doctor was with a client but would see me at six that evening if I wanted to come by the office. I told her I'd be there.

It was after three when a patrolman dropped off a manila envelope. Inside was a sketch showing an aged Henry Whelan. I made half a dozen photocopies, grabbed my coat, tucked the envelope under my arm, and headed for the Clean Sweep offices. If Claudia Oliver had seen Henry, then chances were he'd been hanging around for some time. Angela Bottoms might have seen him, too. I was almost there when I remembered that Angela was out of town.

I hesitated, then continued. Perhaps someone else had seen him. An elderly man with a thatch of white hair, a cowlick that stood straight up and a disgruntled look was manning the desk. He shoved a pair of gold-rimmed glasses down his nose and peered over the tops at me as I entered.

I introduced myself and handed him the sketch. "Have you ever seen this man?"

He pushed the glasses back in place and glanced at it then back at me, his gaze wary. "What's he done?"

I decided to lie. "Nothing that I know of. I'm trying to locate him for his family. They want to help him."

"I've seen him around a time or two."

"Today?"

He shook his head. "Not for a day or two."

"Do you know where he's staying?"

"Nope. You might try the shelters."

I gave him my card. "If you see him, would you give me a call? By the way, what's your name?"

The wariness was back in his eyes. "Why do you want to know?"

"No reason. When will Angela be back?"

"You know Angela?"

"Sure. She left a message on my answering machine that she wanted to see me. Will she be back tomorrow?"

"Not until the end of next week. And my name's Barry. Barry Winters."

"Thanks, Barry. Tell Angela I'll give her a call next week."

I walked back to my office, called Sam, and repeated my conversation with Mr. Winters. He grunted and hung up.

I got in my car and drove to Four Star Cleaners on Queen Anne. The fat man wasn't in sight but the girl was hunched over the sewing machine. She didn't look up until I was beside her.

I slid the picture out and handed it to her. "Was this the man you saw talking to Mrs. Trent?"

She gave a hurried glance over her shoulder, then at the picture. "I don't know," she said, trying to hand the picture back.

"Please, take a closer look. It's important."

After another glance towards the back of the building, she studied the picture. "I'm not sure. It could be. The build is the same and he was wearing the same kinda pants. I didn't get a real good look at his face, but, yeah, it could be."

"Do you think you would recognize him if you saw him again?"

She shrugged. "Maybe. Look, I gotta get back to work."

I got back in the car, and lit a cigarette, trying to decide what to do next. If Henry Whelan had been stalking Maureen, he was sure to know where she lived. I finished the cigarette, snuffed it out, and drove up the hill.

Belle Goodrich wasn't home. It was nearly dark and the drizzle had turned to a fine mist. I walked past the Trent house and knocked on Miss de la Figoniere's door.

If it hadn't been for her size, I wouldn't have recognized her. She was dressed in a high-necked satin hostess gown, and in the dim light, her artfully applied makeup made her look almost youthful. She recognized me and invited me in. I followed her down the hall wishing I had half her grace of movement. Next to her, I felt as large and awkward as a giraffe next to a gazelle. Maybe I'd find time to take ballet lessons one of these days.

She offered me a drink that I refused, then settled on a petite velvet covered chair and motioned me to a seat on the couch and looked at me inquisitively.

I took out the sketch and handed it to her. "Have you ever seen this man in the neighborhood?"

She took her time studying the sketch, then looked up, her black eyes flashing. "Yes. I've seen him a number of times. Who is he?"

I ignored her question and asked, "Have you seen him in the last couple of weeks?"

"Yes. He was across the street just a couple of days ago."

"Could this be the man you saw the morning Mrs. Trent disappeared?"

She laughed, a low musical sound, as she handed the sketch back. "Oh, my dear, no."

"Are you sure?"

"Of course. Didn't I tell you? The man I saw leaving was a black man."

CHAPTER TWENTY

Anson Penman.

The name ripped through my mind like a razor blade through paper. He *was* having an affair with Maureen. Was she blackmailing him? Threatening his political ambitions? Had he killed her?

I slid the sketch back into the envelope, thanked Miss de la Figoniere, and left. The rain had stopped. A good thing because my mind was not on my driving.

Had Anson Penman killed Maureen? Or, was Maureen really on the run and had turned to him for protection? Despite what I'd told Sam, I hadn't really believed Maureen was still alive. Now I began to wonder. Had my gut instinct been wrong?

From Penman, my thoughts skidded to Claudia Oliver. She was in love with Penman and she'd made no effort to hide her dislike for Maureen Trent. Was her jealousy strong enough to drive her to murder? I wanted to know more about both Penman and Oliver. I also wanted to talk with Mark Kiner. According to both his sister and his uncle, Mark Kiner still loved Maureen. Enough to hide her?

It was five minutes till six when I parked beside Dr. Magnuson's office. There was no one in the receptionist's cubicle, but by the time I'd crossed the waiting room, a middle aged woman in a nurse's uniform appeared in the inner door. "Miss Roarke?" she asked. At my nod, she said, "Please come this way. The doctor will see you in his office."

I followed her down the hall and entered the door she indicated and waited until she turned away before closing the door and crossing the room.

Dr. Magnuson glanced up from a paper he was reading and waved me to a chair. He was in his middle sixties, short and on the chubby side, with a round cherubic face. If he'd had a beard to match his white hair, he could have posed for Santa Claus. There was nothing merry about the piercing blue eyes that appraised me.

He straightened in his chair and said, "Miss Roarke, I'm seeing you only because Ian asked me to. I'll tell you the same thing I told him, my patient's files are confidential."

"I understand that, Doctor. Did Mr. Donlevy explain the circumstances?"

"About Maureen being missing? Yes, he did. I'm afraid I fail to see how anything I could tell would be of any assistance in locating her, even if I was willing to break my patient's trust."

"I have only two questions. Both can be answered with a yes or no. If you can do that, I won't press for more."

"Ask your questions and I'll see."

"Was Maureen Trent suffering from any fatal illness?"

Whatever he was expecting, it obviously wasn't that. "No, certainly not."

"Was she pregnant?" I watched him intently for any reaction as I asked the second question.

"Impossible!"

That definitely wasn't the answer I was expecting and it left me stunned. A no answer I could have understood but impossible? And spoken with such emphasis? I wanted to know more but before I could even form another question Dr.

Magnuson shook his head.

"That's all I'm willing to say. Good night, Miss Roarke."

I drove home pondering the implications of the word and the emphatic way it had been uttered. I took the dogs for a long walk trying to make some sense out of all that I'd learned but nothing jelled.

Carmen had left a heaping plate of her fabulous enchiladas in the oven. I retrieved them, spooned sour cream on top and demolished the whole batch. Hunger pangs satisfied, I put all thought of the case out of my mind and spent the hours before bed practicing one of the new pieces of music I'd brought back from Boston. Music is the one thing that can always soothe me. I'll never need booze or drugs as long as I can have music.

Friday morning was foggy but I rode Robin for an hour, showered, changed into a raw silk suit, ate a big breakfast and headed east over the Cascades. Once across Snoqualmie summit, the fog disappeared and only a few high clouds gamboled through the pale cobalt sky. Two hours later, I had located the private hospital where Mark Kiner was a patient.

It didn't look like any hospital I'd ever seen. A number of long, white, one story buildings nestled along a river amid green lawns and flower beds bursting with riotous color. If it hadn't been for the sign in front, I'd have assumed it was a resort.

I was shuffled from one person to another and finally to the Director before I was able to convince them to bend their visiting rules and allow me to interview their patient. I was shown into a small salon containing a couple of couches, set at right angles to each other, and a television set. The television was on but the sound turned was down. I had barely seated myself when the nurse returned, followed by Mark Kiner.

He was short and nearly as rotund as his uncle but the

resemblance ended there. Kiner had a full head of curly brown hair and his eyes were a warm, but vacant brown. He had none of Myron Westover's nervous energy. He crossed the room in slow motion, dropped onto the couch, leaned his head against the back, and closed his eyes.

When I introduced myself, he merely grunted, without opening his eyes. I asked a couple of routine questions that he ignored. Losing patience and wanting to jar him into some kind of response, I asked, "Why did you kill Maureen Trent?"

It worked. His eyes flew open and he sat up. "What?"

"That's better. Have you seen Maureen since the nineteenth of last month?"

"Maureen? No. Kill. You said kill." He leaned forward rubbing his temples with his thumbs. It was like watching a very young child trying to concentrate.

"Maureen has been missing since the morning of the nineteenth of March. Didn't you know?"

"Hell, no."

Some of the vagueness left his eyes. I could see I was finally beginning to get through to him. "When was the last time you saw Maureen?" I asked.

"Not for over three years."

"You did know she was married."

"Yeah. Uncle Myron told me. What do you mean, missing?"

I told him about her disappearance. "She told someone that you had been following her."

"Following her? No, I never followed her. When?"

"Last month. Just before she disappeared."

He shook his head. "I haven't been out of here since just after Christmas."

"Has she been here to visit you? To ask you for help?"

"No." He leaned back again, this time staring at the ceiling. "She wouldn't. Because of the house."

"What house?"

"The one my folks left me. She wanted me to sell it but I wouldn't. That's when she left me."

"She cleaned out your bank account when she left. That must have made you angry."

He waved a hand. "It was just money. She needed it."

"Why?"

He rolled his head until he was looking at me. "She needs money to feel secure. She doesn't trust people, you know. Her folks left her. Ian left her."

"But—"

"Yeah, her folks were killed. They couldn't help it but Maureen still felt abandoned. They left some money but not a whole lot. Ian had to work like hell those first years and pour what money there was into the business to keep it going. He didn't have a lot of time for her. Then she fell in love with some kid during her first year in college. He went off to one of those fancy eastern universities but he played her along for over a year. Came home the first summer and knocked her up, then went back east and married some rich girl. Maureen had an abortion."

"Her brother didn't tell me that."

"He never knew. Look, Maureen was really mixed up. She was like—stunted, you know. Emotionally. People weren't real to her. I mean, she never understood about other people's feeling or cared what they thought about her. Except for Ian. She cared about Ian, cared about his opinion of her. He's Catholic, you know." He turned his attention back to the ceiling. "Who told you I'd been following her?"

"A college friend of hers, Connie Phillips."

192

"That bitch. It figures."

"You know her?"

"Sure. She's a leech. A Goddamned bloodsucking leech."

My disbelief must have shown, for Mark laughed. "Oh, she didn't want money, nothing so simple. The mealy-mouthed little hypocrite. She just wanted to take over Maureen's life, all in the name of *friendship*. With friends like her, Maureen didn't need enemies. Always sucking up, playing the selfless, devoted acolyte ad nauseam. And when that didn't work, she'd pour on the conscience routine, try and make Maureen feel guilty. *Don't you think you're wrong not to tell your brother? Such a sin to carry on your shoulders.*"

His mimicry of Connie Phillips' flat, breathless voice sent a shiver down my spine. "She knew about the abortion?"

"Sure. She made all the arrangements for Maureen, went with her to hold her hand, covered for her. And never let Maureen forget it."

"She seemed so... so innocuous, when I met her," I said. "I would have thought Maureen would have dumped her a long time ago."

"She tried. God, how she tried. Connie's got the hide of a rhinoceros and the tentacles of a octopus." He sat up, rubbing his knuckles. "Connie's a control freak. I've always felt sorry for Mrs. Phillips. The last time I saw her, she was practically a zombie, couldn't open her mouth or make a move without Connie's kindly guidance."

Connie's problems didn't interest me. I concentrated on the rest that Mark had said. So Maureen had had an abortion that her brother knew nothing about. That did interest me. I asked, "Do you know where she went for the abortion? What clinic?"

"No clinic. One of the medical students did it. Butchered

her pretty good, too. Maybe it was a good thing. Maureen would have made a lousy mother."

"Maureen can't have children?" That put a whole new light on the conversation Belle Goodrich had overheard.

"Nah. Like I say, it was probably just as well."

The nurse beckoned from the door. Mark stood up and said, "I gotta go."

I followed them out of the room. "Wait. One more question."

He stopped, waiting, without turning back.

"Does the name Anson Penman mean anything to you?"

"He's Maureen's attorney. Handled all of her real estate deals."

"Were they lovers?"

"That's two questions. No, I don't think so." He shrugged. "But who knows. Or cares."

I watched him shuffle down the hall after the nurse, then went outside into the heat and the sun. I could almost feel sorry for Mark Kiner. Almost.

It was only one o'clock when I dropped down out of the mountains. I thought about Alice Kiner's talk of the masks people hid behind and knew it would be a long time before I would be able to look at any one without wondering what was behind the face they were presenting. I knew I should go to my office, check my messages and dig deeper into Mr. Anson Penman but I was too depressed. I went home.

Carmen had a pot of menudo bubbling on the stove and its redolence started my mouth salivating and my stomach rumbling even though I don't like the Mexican soup. I'm generally easy to please but tripe and hominy are two of my pet hates.

I could hear the vacuum going upstairs but I didn't want to

194

have to put on a happy face for Carmen. I dropped my purse and briefcase in the den, tiptoed back to the kitchen, and raided the refrigerator. I took out a jar of hot, sweet mustard and leftover ham, and made myself a sandwich, sliced an apple and some Swiss cheese and grabbed a can of Coke. Juggling everything, I retreated to the den and closed the door with my heel.

There were three messages on my desk, the first from my mother. I dialed and took a bite of the sandwich.

"Hi, Mom," I mumbled around the food.

"Don't talk with your mouth full. How many times do I have to tell you?" This was said in such an abstracted manner that I knew her mind wasn't on the conversation. "Did you want something, Kerry?"

"Mom, you called me, remember?"

"Oh, yes. You will come to dinner Sunday night, won't you?"

"I'll be there."

"Seven o'clock. Now you be sure to come."

"I will. Promise. See you later."

I hung up, wolfed down the rest of the sandwich, and picked up the message from Ian Donley. I shoved the cheese and apples to the side as I dialed. It wouldn't do to talk to client with my mouth full of food. It wasn't his office number.

His tone was wary when he answered but warmed up considerably when I spoke. "Kerry. I was hoping you would call. Will you have dinner with me tonight?"

The request took me by surprise. He rushed on, covering my hesitancy. "I'd like you to bring me up to date on what you've found out."

"There isn't that much. I can give you a rundown right now."

Now it was his turn to hesitate. "The thing is...I'd just like some company this evening. It's... it's been a rough day and I'm not looking forward to tomorrow..."

"But surely your wife–"

"I'm not married."

"Oh." My heart did a little flip. "You must have close friends–"

"More than I knew. All full of sympathy and understanding and platitudes. God, that's the last thing I need right now. I need someone to talk to, Kerry, really talk. Everyone keeps changing the subject."

I knew what he meant. I remembered all of the friends and neighbors who had crowded the house when Dad died. They had meant well, but their sympathy and pity had been cloying. I had wanted, needed, to talk about Dad, to share stories, to remember to good times Their avoidance of "the painful subject", their kindly meant advice "not to dwell on it", had only driven the loss and pain deeper.

If just listening to him, letting him talk out the hurt would help, it was the least I could do. Perhaps it would help me, too. "Sure," I said. "What time and where?"

"Do you mind coming to my place? The reporters have been hounding me all week. I just can't face them right now."

It wasn't what I expected but I could understand his not wanting to go out in public so I agreed. He told me to come about eight and gave me his address in Mukilteo.

The last message was from Sam. I dialed, wondering if he had located Henry Whelan. He was out when I called but he had left a message. Maureen's car had been found by a couple of teenagers. In the Green River, upstream from Black Diamond.

CHAPTER TWENTY ONE

My heart crowded up in my throat and I had to swallow a couple of times before I could ask, "Her body?"

"You'll have to talk to Detective McCready."

"Do you know where he is?"

She told me Sam was still at the scene and gave me directions. I dashed off a quick note to Carmen that I wouldn't be home for dinner, grabbed my purse, and hurried out. Dozens of questions raced through my mind as I took Highway 18 over Tiger Mountain mentally cursing the construction delays.

The area was cordoned off and I had to park nearly a half a mile away. Walking back in my pumps, I regretted not taking the time to change into slacks and low heeled shoes.

The King County policeman tried to shoo me away but Sam's name carried enough weight to get me through the line. I found Sam leaning against his car watching the river.

"Where's the car?" I asked.

He straightened and turned to face me. "Hi, Kerry. The car is on its way to town so the lab guys can go over it."

"Did you find her body?"

He shook his head. "It wasn't in the car. We've got divers down now but you know this river. It may be months before we find it."

Searchers were pounding the brush on both sides of the river. I hung around until it got too dark for the searchers to

197

continue and the divers gave up for the day. Sam gave me a ride back to my car. I told him about Barry Winters at Clean Sweep and Miss de la Figoniere identifying the picture of Henry Whelan. "Have you done any checking on him?" I asked.

"Yeah. I requested his Triple I from Sacramento. Whelan was picked up in San Diego in January of 1979 for loitering. In 1985, in San Francisco, he was arrested for assault. The charge was reduced to panhandling and creating a public disturbance when the victim failed to press charges."

My gut was churning. "When in 1985?"

He pulled in behind my car, parked, and looked at me. "In March."

"Do you know the victim's name? Was it Marie Brill?"

He continued to look at me without speaking.

"It was, wasn't it?" I asked, my pulse beginning to race. "Wasn't it?"

"Yeah."

"But that didn't stop him," I said, more to myself than to Sam. "He found her and killed her. Now he's still here. He hasn't found Maureen. He's hunting for her. You've got to stop him, Sam."

"Kerry, she's dead."

"Then why is he still here?"

"I don't know, but we'll find him."

"You really will look for him? Question him?"

"Yeah." He reached over and patted my hand.

"What about the mental hospitals? Were you able to find out anything?"

"Not much."

"But he had been admitted?"

"Yeah, on three occasions."

"When was the last time? Three years ago?"

He twisted in the seat and looked at me, his gaze intense. "He was picked up in Redding, California thirty-two months ago and was released just five months ago. How did you know?"

I tried to smile but it didn't quite come off. My lips were too stiff. "Just guessing. He knew about Arthur's marriage. I saw the clipping. There had to be some reason why he wasn't here sooner."

"Kerry, let us take it from here."

"You've reopened the case?"

"Yeah. I guess we have. Go home. Let us handle it now."

I'd be more than happy to leave Henry Whelan to the police but finding Maureen was still my job. That wasn't something Sam would want to hear. "You'll let me know how it's going?" I asked as I climbed out.

"Yeah, sure." The look of concentration he'd been wearing all evening, lightened and the grin he gave me was positively gloating. "See you Sunday night."

I drove home, took a quick shower, selected the prettiest bikini panties and a matching French bra from the hand-made lingerie I'd bought in Boston. Donning fawn colored linen slacks and matching tunic top, I added a gold link belt and gold hoop earrings, dabbed on a little Flora Danica perfume, grabbed a russet colored wool jacket and dashed out.

It took me a while to find his house. I was already late but I took a moment to admire Ian Donlevy's home. It was a modified Queen Anne of mellow brick and cedar, with leaded glass windows facing the street. The curving walk was brick, laid in a herringbone pattern, with a border of yellow and pink primroses interspersed with clumps of white and purple muscari.

Across the street a car door opened and I recognized the man who got out as a reporter for the Seattle Post-Intelligencer. I had no desire to talk to him. I hopped out and hurried up the walk.

Ian must have been watching for me because the door opened before I had a chance to ring the bell. He ushered me in, saying, "I was afraid you'd changed your mind," and quickly slammed the door.

"Something came up."

His hands paused on my arms, my coat half off. I could feel them trembling, as he asked, "About Maureen? Has she been found?"

"No, but–"

"Then we can talk about it after dinner." He hung my coat in the hall closet. "Do you mind coming in the kitchen?"

"Not a bit." I followed him through the entryway and down a short hall. My eyes widened at the size of the kitchen. He led me around a butcher block topped island, as large as most dining room tables, to a breakfast booth set in a box window overlooking the waters of Puget Sound. The table had been set for two with blue place mats and napkins, decorated with nautical flags. "May I get you a glass of wine?"

I shook my head. "I could drink a Coke, if you have one."

He chuckled, a deep masculine sound that made me catch my breath and sent my pulse racing. "Will you settle for some New York Seltzer? Lemon flavor okay?"

"Sounds good."

He brought me the drink in a heavy crystal glass. "Do you mind eating here?"

"I'd love to. This view must be fantastic in the day time."

"It is. It's one of the reasons I bought this house. If you'll excuse me, I'll just finish the salad."

"Can I help with something?"

"Thanks, but I think I have it under control. We're just having steak, baked potatoes, and salad. How do you like your steak?"

"On the rare side of medium."

"A girl after my own heart. It'll be ready in a few minutes."

I sipped the drink, watching him tear lettuce, then slice tomatoes. He looked very much at home in the kitchen and he handled the knife like a professional chef. I was impressed. I love food but I'm not much of a cook. I haven't the patience. I had to remind myself that I made a policy of never getting romantically involved with my clients. A policy I'd had no problem adhering to in the past, but was now in danger of being ignored.

The sound of a boat horn drew my attention back to the window and I watched two ferries crossing paths in the dark water. I concentrated on the lights twinkling on the dark bulk of Whidbey Island.

He brought the steaks on heavy blue and white plates, still sizzling from the Jenn-Aire broiler. One look at the potato on the side piled high with butter, sour cream, bacon bits, and chives, and I knew I'd have to spend a week on the Nautilus.

We ate in silence, giving our full attention to the food. At last, completely sated, I leaned back in the booth and watched him finish the last of his steak. The only thing lacking was an after dinner cigarette.

He whisked away the dishes and returned with a heavy glass ashtray. I looked up at him in surprise. He grinned and said, "You are a smoker, aren't you?"

"How did you know?"

"Your office. You had an ashtray on your desk. Go ahead and smoke."

My liking for him shot up another notch. No doubt about it, I could go for this man in a big way. I lit up while he slid into the booth.

"What happened today?"

"The police found Maureen's car." I went on to tell him all I knew and all I suspected about Henry Whelan. I didn't tell him my suspicion that his sister might still be alive. In my heart I didn't believe it and I didn't want to raise false hopes.

"Then you don't think Arthur killed Maureen?"

"No. I'm reasonably sure, at least in my own mind, that Henry Whelan killed Maureen. Buffy, too. But Arthur couldn't know that. From what Mrs. Montgomery and Seth Steiner told me, Arthur believed Buffy had left him and he took it hard. The thought that Maureen had left him, too, was too much for him to face. I think that's what his message to you meant."

"God, if you're right, what kind of hell must he have been going through. If I had only realized..."

I listened for several hours while he talked through his grief and guilt. I felt doubly guilty because the Maureen he talked about, the kid sister, was not the same person as the one I'd been investigating. I briefly considered fudging on my written report, then shrugged the thought aside. The things I'd found out about Maureen Donlevy Trent were bound to come out. There was no way I could spare him that further pain.

I longed to hold him, comfort him, but couldn't make the first move. We were both physically and mentally exhausted by the time he glanced at his watch and said, "My God, I've kept you up all night."

At the door, he helped me into my coat, then turned me to

face him. Sliding a hand under my chin, he tilted my face up and kissed me lightly on the lips. "Thank you, Kerry," he whispered and kissed me again, not quite so gently, his arms folding me against him.

The thrill that ran through me went all the way down to my toes. I was more than a little breathless as I backed away. "I'll see you later today."

He dropped his arms. I reached up and laid my hand against his cheek for a moment, then opened the door and hurried down the walk before I was tempted to break my rule of not getting involved with a client.

I was hot and bothered all the way home and my sleep the rest of the night was filled with wet dreams.

I slept late and woke up in a foul mood. Not even my daily ride improved my spirits. I ate the breakfast Carmen put before me without tasting it.

My day certainly wasn't improved when Sam called just before noon. Copies of Whelan's fingerprints had come through from California on AFIS and they matched prints taken from the outside of the passenger door and mirror of Maureen's car. However, none of Whelan's prints had been found inside the car. They had not located either Maureen's body or Whelan.

CHAPTER TWENTY TWO

Carmen had been tiptoeing around me and I could almost hear her sigh of relief when I went upstairs. I showered, washed and dried my hair, then opened my closet.

I own only one black suit, a light wool at least ten years old, with a fitted jacket and pleated skirt. Mary Sue tells me no one wears black to funerals anymore but Mom has drilled her ideas of proper behavior into me and I still have a difficult time disregarding them. I pulled the suit out of the back of the closet and dug through hat boxes until I found a black felt hat. I love hats and I'm glad they're beginning to come back in style. I pulled out a pair of pumps, then changed my mind and put on a pair black flats. This time of year the ground at the cemetery was likely to be soggy.

The sun was shining when I left the house, but knowing Seattle weather, I tossed an umbrella in the car, just in case. Saturday traffic on I-90 is mostly east bound, so I made good time all the way to Ballard.

I'd never been in a Lutheran church, and unsure of what to expect, I slipped into a seat in the rear. It was a small church, hardly larger than a chapel, and seemed stark and bare compared to the Catholic church I'd attended with my father or even the synagogue where Mom has gone since Dad died. The front of the church was banked with flowers, their perfume hanging heavy on the air.

The chapel didn't seem so empty by the time the fifty or so

mourners were seated. The only person I recognized was Simone de la Figoniere. She was seated half way to the altar on the center aisle. She and I were the only ones dressed in black. I'd wondered if Maureen's "best friend" Connie Phillips would be there. She wasn't.

Ian's face was pale and set as he took his place in the front row. He looked so alone and forlorn, I considered moving up to sit beside him but before I could change seats the minister entered.

It was a beautiful service despite being short and simple. Halfway through the eulogy the door behind me was cracked open, distracting me, but it closed before I got more than a glimpse of khaki pants and plaid flannel shirt.

When the service was over, I waited a few moments, trying to catch a glimpse of Ian, but he disappeared out a side door and I joined the throng exiting the church. The bright sunshine had disappeared behind a screen of gray clouds and a chill breeze off the Sound had sprung up. It smelled of rain and the sea and it washed away the heavy fragrance of the flowers that had begun to stifle me.

Burial was to take place at Washelli Cemetery. I saw Ian being ushered into a limousine. Our glances met for an instant and his eyes brightened, then the mortuary assistant shut the car door and I turned away.

The procession was already forming. I'd parked in the far corner of the parking lot and I hurried across the asphalt. Unlocking the door, I glanced across the top of the car. In that instant, the clouds parted momentarily and a shaft of sunlight lit up the parking lot like a spotlight, and I saw him clearly.

I froze, staring. Henry Whelan was sitting in a battered and rusted red Ford pickup.

He must have felt my stare for he turned his head and our

glances locked. For an instant his eyes widened in surprise, then flared in anger. Before I could move, he had thrown the truck in gear and backed out of the parking space, nearly colliding with the hearse that was just beginning to pull away from the church.

I dived into my car, and without bothering with my seat belt, started the motor and pulled out, weaving between the other cars jockeying to form the procession. I had a brief glimpse of Ian's shocked face as I raced by the limousine and swung into the street.

The red Ford was speeding away a block and a half ahead of me. I tromped on the accelerator and felt the power of the big engine unleash. I was within half a block of him when my brain took over. What was I going to do if I caught him?

I had no authority to arrest him. Unless Sam had come up with something else, there was nothing to tie Henry Whelan to the disappearance of Maureen Trent, except his fingerprints on her car. Or, for that matter, to connect him with any of the other missing women. I eased back, and keeping him in sight, let a couple of other cars move in between us.

It didn't work. He knew he was being followed. He raced up and down several side streets, cut through a parking lot but I stayed with him. Where the hell were the police when you needed them?

I needed Sam. Henry Whelan's fingerprints on the outside of Maureen's car would be reason enough for Sam to question him. For the first time I regretted not having a car phone. Monday I'd damn well have one installed.

I followed him across the Fremont Bridge, along Lake Union, nearly lost him in the traffic around the Seattle Center as he cut back west, and again near the Pike Place Market. The rain came lightly as I followed him up First Hill and around

Seattle University, then in torrents as we wove around through the Central District.

Suddenly, he was gone.

I double-parked and sat, drumming my fingers on the steering wheel, thinking. He was close. I knew it, could feel it. I'd find him. I'd grown up in this area and knew it well. Correction, had known it well. It had changed in the years since Mom had sold the liquor store and we'd moved away, but not that much. He'd gone to ground but I'd find him.

An angry horn blast startled me, jarring me back to reality. The last thing I wanted was to come face to face with Henry Whelan, but I did want find where he was staying. Then Sam could take over. I threw the car in gear and drove down the street searching the curbs and driveways for the red Ford.

I cruised all of the streets within a six-block range of where I'd last seen him but there was no red pickup. I found a parking spot almost in front of the drug store we'd patronized in the past and dashed inside. The phone booth was still in the back but the druggist was new and the sales clerk was a young black girl in a mini-skirt and dreadlocks. I wondered what had happened to Mrs. Kovak. As a kid I'd come in often. Mrs. Kovak had always slipped me a piece of penny candy and allowed me to read the comic books. Comic books were forbidden in our house.

I called Sam's office but he wasn't around. I left a message giving the description and license number of Whelan's pickup and where I'd lost him. I tried Sam's apartment, and as a last resort, tried Mom. There was no answer either place.

Back in the car, I began cruising the alleys and back streets without success. Either he wasn't in the area or he had rented a garage.

It was full dark and still raining when I started a second

swing through the alleys. I knew I should wait for the police but adrenaline was pumping and I was mad, not stupid. I didn't intend to challenge Whelan, but I did want to know where he'd gone to earth.

I parked at the head of each block, and carrying my umbrella and powerful flashlight, walked down the block checking all the garages on the right then back to the car checking the ones on the left. Then I'd drive to the next block and repeat the process. Almost every other house had a garage. By the time I'd covered every garage in eleven blocks, my shoes were soaked, my feet felt like lumps of frozen hamburger, and I was chilled to the bone. Twice I'd been scared shitless; once when a drunk stumbled out from behind a shed to beg for money and once by a prowling cat.

When I got out of my car to walk the twelfth block, I was tired, hungry and depressed, but too stubborn and too dumb to give up. At least the rain had stopped. The damp air intensified the stench of rotting garbage, mildew, human urine, and animal feces. I carried my umbrella furled, knowing the rain would start again.

He erupted from behind a pile of boxes like a stone from a slingshot. I caught the first hint of movement out of the corner of my eye and threw myself to the side. If my nerves hadn't been stretched taut, I would have been dead.

The blow aimed for my head smashed down on my left arm. I heard rather than felt the bone snap. The force of the blow sent me spinning to the ground, my flashlight flew out of my hand, bounced and landed on a plastic trash sack, it's beam lancing upward, back-lighting the scene.

I scrambled to my knees as Whelan raised the piece of angle iron for another blow. The fingers of my right hand automatically tightened around the umbrella handle and I lunged upward thrusting the umbrella like a fencing foil with all my strength. The tip caught him in the solar plexus and he doubled over, dropping the piece of iron.

I surged to my feet and backed away, the umbrella held in the en garde position. I risked a glance over my shoulder. My car was a good hundred feet away and locked. No escape there.

Whelan picked up the piece of iron and straightened. The flashlight beam played on his face, accentuating the fanatical glitter of his sunken eyes. He moved towards me, slowly, inexorably.

For a moment I was frozen by the almost hypnotic intensity of his stare. He shifted the iron in his hand and the spell was broken. I backed away in a fencing stance, shuffling, afraid of falling on the slime underfoot. My left arm, beginning to throb painfully, dangled uselessly.

He poked the iron at me, almost playfully. I parried with the umbrella, jabbing the point into his armpit. He winced, paused, and lunged forward with a quick swipe that shattered the spine of the umbrella.

I threw the bent remains in his face and did the only thing I could. I turned and ran, screaming at the top of my lungs.

He pounded after me, his footsteps echoing loudly in my ears. The end of the alley was in sight but I knew I'd never make it. On my right, a yard light flashed on, and above the thundering of my heart, I heard voices. Whelan's heavy breathing sounded harsh in my ears. I could almost feel his hot breath on my neck.

My foot came down on something slick and I slid off balance, my right arm windmilling. Something struck my head and the world exploded in a psychedelic swirl.

209

CHAPTER TWENTY THREE

Instinctively, I curled into a fetal position, my right arm curved protectively over my head. The world blurred, shifted, stopped moving, but the alley was still lit with flashing blue and red lights.

Footsteps pounded and I cringed, but they drummed past me and raced down the alley. Shouts and the excited babble of voices penetrated the fog in my brain. I opened my eyes wider, willing my stomach to settle down. Swollen feet in a pair of muddy bedroom slippers shuffled into view and a gentle hand touched my arm.

"Lady, you all right?"

I lowered my arm and looked up into concerned brown eyes in a wrinkled chocolate face. I nodded and wished I hadn't. The world began spinning again and my stomach heaved. Calloused hands, with finger joints swollen and deformed, helped me to sit up, then held me as I vomited. My good samaritan extracted a man's handkerchief from the pocket of her robe and gently wiped my face.

"Thanks," I muttered, struggling to get my feet under me. I gasped and closed my eyes as pain shot up my arm and mingled with the pain in my head. I gave up trying to stand.

Gritting my teeth to hold back the nausea, I opened my eyes and looked around.

In the flashing lights from the patrol car, the alley looked like something out of a horror movie. Figures, indistinct in the shadows, the flashing lights playing red and blue on their features, looked like gaping specters. My Samaritan disappeared into the throng.

Henry Whelan emerged from the darkness, arms handcuffed behind his back, a police officer gripping him on either side. As he passed, he glared down at me and shouted, "The work of the Lord shall not be thwarted. Vengeance is mine."

He was shoved in the back of the patrol car and one of the officers came to kneel beside me, assuring me that an ambulance was on the way. I gave him a brief statement, suggested he contact Sam McCready, and was relieved when the ambulance arrived.

It took a lot of argument, but after the officer retrieved my purse with my insurance card from my car, I finally convinced the ambulance driver to take me to Overlook Hospital instead of Harborside. Harborside is a great hospital with an outstanding trauma center but its emergency room is always overloaded with the indigent and its staff overworked. I had no desire to lay on a gurney for hours, waiting to have my arm set. Fortunately, I can afford excellent insurance.

By the time I'd had a jillion x-rays and my arm set, I was more than ready to settle into a hospital bed for the night and sleep. Unfortunately, the nurses kept waking me up every few minutes to make sure I hadn't slipped into a coma.

Sam arrived along with my breakfast tray. He lounged against the window while the aide raised my bed and arranged the tray. Dry toast and definitely dyed...with yellow food coloring. *Yuuk*! Dyed egg whites did nothing to stimulate my appetite but I sipped the juice while Sam paced and lectured me on my foolhardiness. He was as upset as I'd ever seen him.

I listened, out of courtesy, until he ran down, then I had to ask, "Have you questioned Whelan?"

"Of course we've questioned him. Half the damned night."

"Well?"

"So far all he's done is misquote scripture."

"What about Maureen?"

"Nothing."

"You aren't going to let him go?"

"Hell, no. Not yet, anyway. We'll do a lineup and see if that French woman and the people from Clean Sweep can identify him. I'm trying to set it up for tomorrow morning."

"Don't forget the girl from the cleaners. She saw someone approach Maureen the morning she disappeared."

"Yeah." He patted my shoulder. "I had your car driven home. They tell me the doc will be around about ten and he'll probably let you go home. I'll be back to pick you up."

He grinned, pulled a plastic bag out of his pocket, and tossed it in my lap. "You might want to keep that for a souvenir. Doc says it probably kept you from a cracked skull."

I peered at the battered, mud encrusted remains of my black felt hat and burst out laughing.

It was almost straight up noon by the time I'd been examined, completed the paper work, and was finally allowed to leave. I'd have looked more at home in Pioneer Square than Bellevue when I walked out of the hospital. My black suit was stained and torn and definitely headed for the ragbag.

I glanced out of the corner of my eye at Sam's set face as he drove me home. His jaw clenched and unclenched and the knuckles of his hand gripping the steering wheel were white. I cracked a hospital joke, trying to lighten the atmosphere.

He pulled onto the shoulder, slammed the car in park, and turned to face me, his face mottled with anger. "It's all a joke to you, isn't it?" His voice was low and rough. "You get your kicks playing at being the big, tough detective."

His attack startled me. "Sam—"

"Just shut up." His disdainful gazed burned as it raked me. "Look at you. Do you have any idea how upset your mother is? Do you care that she's been up all night, out of her mind with worry?"

I opened my mouth but he held up a hand. "No, by God, for once you're going to listen to me. It's time you grew up and stopped playing games."

My own anger was rising. "I'm not playing games. I take my work seriously."

"Like hell you do. Look at that office of yours. It's a joke, a set out of a thirties grade B movie. You run around acting like a character out of one of those pulp detective magazines. You're a joke."

"I am a *good* detective. I am. I am." Hurt and anger warred in my breast. I swallowed trying to hold back the tears that threatened. How dare he talk to me like this?

"You could be, Kerry, if you'd stop playing at it and get serious. He heaved a heavy sigh and his voice softened. "You have good instincts and you're a good investigator but you've got to stop playing around. What you pulled last night was plain stupid. You could have gotten yourself killed."

He pulled back onto the freeway. I stared out at the passing scenery without seeing any of it and wisely kept my mouth shut. I'd never seen Sam so worked up and didn't want another tongue-lashing. We rode in an uncomfortable silence the rest of the way. Sam walked me to the kitchen door, mumbled that he'd see me later, and took off.

Carmen took one look at me as I walked in the door and crossed herself, then dashed up the stairs ahead of me. They

213

had insisted on bathing me at the hospital but after having to wear my dirty clothes home, I didn't feel clean. I wanted a nice hot shower.

Carmen helped me undress, wrapped the cast in plastic bags and rubber bands, and insisted on shampooing my hair, all the while muttering maledictions in Spanish that I pretended not to hear or understand.

We found an old set of sweats, cut off the left sleeve, and worked me into them. Worked is the operative word. I was utterly exhausted by the time we had my body clean and clothed. I looked longingly at the bed, but I knew if I lay down, I'd never get up in time for dinner at Mom's.

Thinking of dinner made me realize I was starving. I sat in the kitchen while Carmen warmed a bowl of her homemade tomato soup and grilled a cheese sandwich. After I'd eaten, I stretched out on the couch in the living room. Carmen brought me a cup of hot chocolate and insisted on wrapping me in an afghan.

I stared out the window at the leaden sky. It looked as gray and depressed as I felt. Sam's words rang in my ears and I tried to shut them out by concentrating on the case.

Sam had Whelan in custody. They'd break the crazy bastard sooner or later; learn where he'd dumped Maureen's body. The case would be closed. I should be feeling relieved but I wasn't. Something about the case still didn't feel right. Like an itch between the shoulder blades that you just can't reach, it wouldn't let me rest. I tried to concentrate but my mind refused to settle down. It kept flitting like a bee on uppers, unable to settle anywhere. The exertion and the sleepless night finally caught up with me and I slept.

When I awoke, the room was dark except for one table lamp on the other side of the room. Mom was sitting in a chair across from me, staring out into the night. My legs were tangled in the afghan and I struggled to free them. My body weighed a ton, my muscles uncoordinated and uncooperative, and the cast kept getting in the way.

Mom got me untangled and I sat up, reaching for a cigarette. She lit it for me and began her usual harangue but I could tell she was speaking from force of habit, neither her heart nor her mind were in it. I listened without hearing, while the fog in my brain slowly dissipated.

When she began to run down, I interrupted. "What's the matter, Mom?"

"What? Oh. Sam called. He won't make it out to dinner tonight."

She was twisting her hands in her lap, something she never does. I reached over and gripped them with my good hand. "Come on, Mom. What gives?"

"Sam should be here."

"Hey, come on. He's questioning a murder suspect. As long as you've known Sam, you should know the demands of his job. This isn't the first time he's had to break a date. It's never bothered you before."

"But this is different. He's never asked me to marry him before." Her mouth snapped shut and she gave me a look I couldn't read. Fear? Anxiety? Embarrassment? Surely not.

Whatever it was, it didn't bother me. Joy bubbled through me and I jumped up, hugging Mom. "Sam proposed? That's great. When's the wedding?"

Mom freed herself from my embrace, stood up, and moved to the window. "I haven't said yes."

That set me back on my heels. "Why not? Don't you love him?"

She gave a helpless little shrug. "I don't know. It's...it's all so sudden."

I couldn't help laughing. "Mom, he's been courting you for twenty years!"

"Kerry! How can you say that?"

"Because it's true. Sam fell for you as soon as he met you. Why do you think he's been coming around all these years?" I took her hand. "You do care for him, don't you?"

"I...I like him."

"Is that all?"

"Well, maybe more than just like. But I never really thought about marrying again."

"Then it's time you did."

One hand fluttered helplessly. "It's so…so inappropriate. It's not like I am a young woman. I'm fifty-four years old. It's ridiculous."

"What's ridiculous about falling in love? And what has age to do with anything?"

"He's younger than I am."

"Oh, for heaven's sake. He can't be more than a couple of years younger. What difference does that make?"

"Three years."

I laughed. "Well, I'd still hardly call that robbing the cradle. Besides, you don't look anywhere near your age. I think it's wonderful."

She looked up at me. "You... you wouldn't mind?"

I laughed again and squeezed her hand. "Mom, I think it would be great. And I can't think of anyone I'd rather have for a stepfather. You and Sam were made for each other."

We talked a while longer and by the time Mom went home, I hoped it wouldn't be long before she said yes to Sam. I went to bed with my head too full of wedding plans to think about Maureen Trent or Henry Whelan.

I slept late the next morning and woke in a more cheerful mood. It lasted until just after lunch when Sam called. They had found a cache of photos hidden in the doorframe of the pickup. Pictures of five women, either dead or unconscious. Each had been set afire. Confronted with the pictures, Henry Whelan had admitted killing Belinda Trent, Marie Brill, Abigail Steiner, Peggy Lockman, and Corinne Lockman. However, he denied killing Maureen Trent.

"He admits he planned to kidnap and kill her, too. He tried to grab her that morning in front of the cleaners but she drove off before he could make his move. He's been hunting for her since then but hasn't located her."

"Do you believe him?" I asked.

"Yeah. He's upset about it. Feels he's failed in what he calls "*the Lord's work*." Says God told him to punish the sinner's by taking an eye for an eye, only he says a wife for a wife. The guy's completely bonkers, but I think he's telling the truth about the Trent woman. No reason for him to lie."

"Then she may still be alive but in hiding." I didn't really believe it. If Henry Whelan hadn't killed Maureen Trent, then someone else had.

CHAPTER TWENTY FOUR

I hung up and sat for a long time staring down at the top of my desk trying to get my thoughts in order, waiting in vain for inspiration to hit. My brain simply didn't want to function. Perhaps it was my body's way of shielding itself or perhaps it was the painkillers the doctor had given me. For whatever reason, I simply couldn't concentrate.

Finally I gave up, dictated a report to date, and called Mary Sue to pick it up. I thought about calling Ian. I owed him an explanation for my rapid and unorthodox departure from the church, but it wasn't something I wanted to explain over the phone and I didn't feel up to seeing him. Besides, my arm was beginning to ache like hell.

I threw out the rest of the pain pills, took a couple of aspirins, went upstairs, and took a nap. I got up long enough to eat the dinner Carmen prepared, watched a couple of sitcoms on television without really seeing them, and went back to bed.

Tuesday dawned bright and sunny and by the time I'd taken the dogs for a short walk, my mind, as well as my lungs, felt clear. Sometime during the night several bits of data I'd picked up had floated to the surface of my brain. There were two people I wanted to talk to. Maureen was dead. She'd been killed on Friday, March 19th, and I was reasonably sure I knew who'd killed her. I needed to verify a couple of things, then I could call Sam.

I called Ian and asked him to meet me at my office at five.

He was upset but I promised to explain everything. It wasn't something I was going to enjoy.

Carmen helped me into a pair of brown gabardine slacks and ankle boots, then maneuvered a brown silk smock with wide sleeves over the cast. The cuff wouldn't button so we used double sided tape to fasten it to the bottom of the cast. She cinched the blouse at the waist with a wide leather belt and I added a heavy velvet vest for warmth before Carmen rigged my arm into its sling.

After a half a dozen fruitless tries, I gave up on fastening my seat belt, decided to risk a ticket, and headed for town. I'd missed the morning rush hour traffic and made good time through downtown Seattle and into the Rainier Valley.

Claudia Oliver was at her desk when I walked in, and if looks could kill, I'd have been mortally wounded the second I walked in the room. I ignored her and threw open the door to the private office before she could stand up.

Anson Penman was scribbling on a yellow pad and didn't look up until I slammed the door. He started to rise, then slumped back in his chair as I asked, "Did Maureen hold a mortgage on Mark Kiner's house?"

"I don't have to give you any information."

"No, you don't." I toed a chair closer to the desk and sat down. "I know all about Maureen's real estate deals and I know you handled all of the legal work. If your dealings with Maureen become public knowledge, you can kiss your political career goodbye. Level with me and I'll do my best to keep you out of it. Otherwise I'll make dammed sure there is a full investigation."

He leaned back and cocked his head, his face settling into lines of disdain. But he couldn't hide the tiny muscle twitch under his left eye. We played eye chicken, a game I'm very good at, for several minutes before he broke and looked away. "I don't know what you're talking about."

"Sure you do. You know all about the little side games Maureen was playing while she was at Fiedler-McLaren. You advised her, took care of all the legal work. You've been helping her in her latest scams. I'll ask you again, did Maureen hold a mortgage on Mark Kiner's house?"

"No." There was a fine line of sweat along his hairline and his voice was lifeless.

"Any liens or mortgages on Myron Westover?"

"No."

"Alice Kiner?"

"No."

"Connie Phillips?"

"No."

His answers shook me for a moment, then I knew. "Just a few more questions. How many mortgages did Maureen foreclose on in the last few months? How many pieces of property has she sold?"

He just looked at me, and for a moment, I didn't think he was going to answer. Finally he sighed and said, "She foreclosed on fourteen. Eleven are in escrow and should close within a month. Deals on the other three fell through. I told her she was trying to move too fast but she wouldn't listen."

"She was getting ready to split. Why?"

"She was getting antsy. Someone had been following her."

"Who?"

He shook his head. "I don't know. She didn't know, either."

"But she must have had some suspicion. Didn't she give you any hint?"

220

"At first she thought it was a guy she'd lived with for a while. Thought it was his way of trying to get her back. Took it as a big joke."

"What made her change her mind?"

"I'm not sure. She had a fight with her husband. She thought for a while that he was having her followed. But then she changed her mind. I don't know why. Maybe... I don't know. Anyway, she decided to divorce him."

"What were you doing at her house the morning she disappeared?"

"I don't know what you're talking about."

I leaned forward. "Bullshit! You were seen leaving the house early that morning. Were you having an affair?"

"No. No. Nothing like that. Maureen called me just before midnight and wanted me to bring the divorce papers and some other things by. Wanted them by six o'clock. I dropped them off. That's all. I swear it."

"Neither the police or her brother found any divorce papers when the searched the house."

"They're probably in her secret files. When they were remodeling, she had a secret file built into the left side wall of the closet in the room she used as an office."

"If she was planning to divorce Arthur, and she wasn't having an affair, why was she afraid of being followed?"

"She thought the guy was crazy."

"She knew who was following her?"

"No, but she said he was spooky. Look, Maureen Trent was a first class bitch. She didn't have a friend in the world except that kooky broad she went to school with and Maureen was getting ready to screw her. I think she felt at least one of her chickens was coming home to roost. I won't say she was exactly scared, Maureen was too sure of herself for that, but I think she thought she'd played out her string here and was looking for greener pastures."

"I know she transferred over a hundred thousand dollars before she disappeared, but that's not much of a stake in today's economy."

"It's peanuts. When the escrows closed, she'd have had another two million or so."

I needed more answers. "Did she leave a will?"

"If she did, I didn't draw it up for her."

I had what I'd come for. Claudia Oliver rushed in as soon as I opened the door. She had his head cradled to her breast as I went out. She might get him yet, but if she did, she wouldn't be getting much.

I drove north using surface streets, using the extra time to put my thoughts in order. I made three stops. The first was a gun shop where I bought a Smith and Wesson Model 469 9mm automatic with 12 round capacity, two extra clips, a shoulder holster, an ankle holster and filled out all the paper work. I'd have to wait a week to pick it up, but that was okay, I'd need a lot of time on the firing range before I'd feel up to handling it. From now on I wanted something more than the little .22 target pistol in my safe at home.

My second stop was to purchase a cellular phone for my car. While they were installing it, I took a cab to the Trent house. Using a set of lock picks disguised in a manicure case, I let myself in.

Most of the rooms were done in a vaguely nautical theme, using predominantly blues and whites. All but one room. It was done in earth tones and furnished with antiques, including an old roll top desk. I found the secret file cabinet in the closet, right where Penman said it would be. The lock presented no problems.

When I'd finished reading the documents, I put them back, and re-locked the cabinet. I'd let Ian "find" them later. The records of all her dirty little deals were there. I knew Ian would want to be alone when he read them. I used the phone to call a cab. Re-locking the front door, I waited on the porch. I now knew who had killed Maureen and why.

My car was ready when I got back. I used my new phone to call Sam and tell him where I was going and why. I hung up before he could argue. A few minutes later I was in Lynnwood, pulling into the Phillips' gravel drive. The rose bushes were loaded with blooms, but for once, I didn't find their scent pleasing.

I parked in front of the house, climbed the steps, and knocked but no one answered. A battered Volkswagen beetle was parked at the edge of the gravel, pointed towards the street. Using a handkerchief and twisting the shank under the doorknob, I tried the front door and found it locked. Where was Mrs. Phillips? I tried peering in but the shades had been drawn on the front windows.

Leaving the porch, I circled the house but could see nothing. All of the shades had been drawn. I tried the back door, but it, too, was locked. I hesitated, knowing I should wait for Sam, but I had to know. Using my picks, I opened the door. The fetor of urine and feces and death hit me in the face. I pulled out the handkerchief again and covered my nose.

I found them in the front bedroom. I had to cross the room and tap Connie on the shoulder before she became aware of my presence.

I doubt if she recognized me. The eyes she turned towards me were unfocused and vacant. Her nasal whine was so low I had to bend over to catch her words. "She said she was ready to go, but I won't let her. I told her I'd always take care of her.

I will, too. I'll never let her go. Do you hear, Mama? I won't let you go."

I left her there, crouched in a puddle of urine and feces, beside the bed and backed out of the room. Connie Phillips wasn't going anywhere and her mother was already gone. I went outside, leaving the door open and walked back to the garden plot. The plastic canvas had blown to the ground and the rototiller and garden cart were still wet from the recent rains. I knew better than to touch anything. I was still staring at the recently turned earth when Sam drove in.

Before he could speak, I nodded towards the house and said, "The back door's open."

I knew my face must be as green as I felt, for after one look at me, he headed for the house. I waited by the garden while he went inside, then came out and used his car radio.

When he came back, I asked, "How long has Mrs. Phillips been dead?"

"I'd say the old woman's been dead at least a couple of days, probably more. The autopsy will tell us. The Lynnwood police are on their way. Did you talk to the girl?"

"Not really. She's obviously around the bend. How did Mrs. Phillips die?"

He shrugged. "That will be for the medical examiner to decide. I didn't see any signs of trauma."

I gestured toward the plowed ground. "You'll find Maureen Trent buried here or under the roses."

Units from the Lynnwood Police Department, Snohomish County Sheriff's Department, and the King County Police arrived. I sat in my car, chain smoking, watching them go about their jobs. I waited until they found Maureen's body in the garden patch, then drove back downtown. I wasn't looking forward to seeing Ian. Not with what I had to tell him, but it

224

was time he knew the truth about his sister.

He was pacing the corridor when I arrived. His eyebrows shot up when he saw the cast. "My God, what happened to you?"

Without answering, I unlocked the door, then locked it after him. I didn't want any interruptions.

He tried to put an arm around me but I shrugged it away. "Sit down, Ian. This could take awhile." I walked behind my desk and sat down without looking at him. "This isn't going to be easy, so please, let me tell it my way, then I'll answer your questions."

He dropped into the client chair, his hands clenched tightly on the arms. I kept my gaze glued to his hands as I told him about seeing Henry Whelan at the funeral, glossing over, as much as possible, the fight in the alley and finishing with Whelan's confession to murdering the women.

I watched his hands curl into fists. "Maureen's dead? He killed her?"

"She's dead, but no, he didn't kill her. He would have. Planned to. Someone else killed her first."

"Who?" The word came out in a hoarse whisper.

"Connie Phillips."

"Connie? That's impossible. Connie was Maureen's best friend. They were like sisters."

"I've just come from Connie's place. They dug up your sister's body just before I left."

"But why? Why would Connie kill her?"

"Because Connie's mother, Agnes, had mortgaged her property to pay for Connie's education. The mortgage was held by Fiedler-McLaren."

I looked at him then. "Did you know that Maureen was forced to resign her position at Fiedler-McLaren or face prosecution?"

His face paled but his voice was steady. "Are you sure?"

"Yes. Your sister had been involved in a number of unethical, if not illegal, activities. Anson Penman had helped her set up a series of dummy companies."

I told him about the way she'd taken Mark Kiner to the cleaners. "She funneled the money she stole from Mark and the kickbacks she'd received while at Fiedler-McLaren through the dummy companies and used the money to buy up mortgages that were beginning to default. Mortgages Fiedler-McLaren were happy to get out from under, although I doubt they would have sold to her if they'd known who they were dealing with."

My head was beginning to ache and I wanted this over with. There was no easy way to say it. "When Connie had to quit her job to take care of her mother, they had a hard time meeting the mortgage payments. Their savings were gone; they were living hand to mouth. Maureen knew this when she bought up the mortgage. She bided her time. That's a big piece of ground. Perfect for development. And when she found a developer willing to pay big bucks, she started foreclosure proceedings. Connie and her mother would have been out on the street. No money, no place to go."

"I don't believe it."

"It's true, Ian. Copies of the documents, letters from Connie to Maureen asking for her help, they're all in the filing cabinet in your sister's office." I told him all I had learned about his sister and how to find the secret files.

He stood up, nearly knocking the chair over. "What does Connie say?"

"I don't know. She's... in no condition to be questioned, at the moment. They've taken her to Harborside. The forensic team was still at the scene when I left. I'll include whatever I can find out in my final report."

"Maureen?"

"They will have to do an autopsy."

He took a deep breath and struggled to pull himself together. "What do I do now?"

"Contact Detective McCready. He'll know who you'll need to talk to in Snohomish County."

He turned and walked out the door. I sat for a long time, then reluctantly roughed out letters to Dr. Steiner, Dale Lockman, and Elliot Brill and left them for Mary Sue to type.

I drove home, wishing for once, that I was a drinker. I'd have gotten plastered. Liquor has never been a means of escape for me. I always get sick before I can get stoned.

Only the dogs were there to greet me. I petted them but my heart wasn't in it. I turned on the television, just for the noise. It didn't help. I turned it off then wandered through the house unable to settle down.

It was nearly midnight when Sam came. He looked as exhausted as I felt. He helped himself to a can of Coors and drank half of it before he sat down.

"What made you suspect the Phillips woman?" he asked.

"A nightmare. I dreamed I was sitting on the patio. You and Mom were barbecuing steaks and talking about me. I tried to talk but you both ignored me as if I wasn't there. Then I realized you were using the past tense. When I woke up, I remembered my interview with Connie. She talked of Maureen in the past tense."

"That doesn't mean someone's dead. Hell, I'm always talking about what a great guy Jerry McGovern was. He isn't dead, I just don't see him since he retired and moved to Arizona."

"I know, but it made me start thinking of other people who might have wanted Maureen dead. She took Mark Kiner for a bundle and walked out on him over a house. The shit she pulled at Fiedler-McLaren all involved real estate. If Anson Penman wasn't Maureen's lover, then he was probably involved in whatever rig she was running. When I went to see him this morning, I asked about liens and mortgages. He denied any knowledge when I mentioned Kiner and Westover. He denied Connie Phillips, too, but he hesitated just the tiniest bit."

"You knew he was lying."

"No. He was telling the truth. The property was in *Agnes Phillips'* name. Right answer, wrong question, but it tipped me off. Connie was obviously devoted to her mother, at least in her own sick way."

"That was all?"

"No. There was the pregnancy."

"What pregnancy?"

"Belle Goodrich overheard an argument over having a baby, remember? Connie said that Arthur wanted a child but Maureen didn't. That part I'm sure was true. I think it's why Maureen was divorcing him. But Connie said it was because the doctor had told Maureen it would be dangerous. That was a lie. Connie knew Maureen couldn't have children because of a botched abortion. Connie had held the threat of exposure over Maureen all these years."

"But abortions aren't that uncommon."

"Maureen was Catholic. She might not have taken her Christianity seriously in her business dealings, but I doubt if she could face being excommunicated from the church. Also, she did love her brother. She left him everything in her will. Maybe she felt it was one sin he couldn't forgive.

"Mrs. Trent went to the Phillips house that morning. I

wonder why."

I shrugged. "We'll probably never know for sure. The sale of the Phillips property was in escrow and do to close in a few weeks. The money was to be paid into an account in the Cayman Islands. Maureen had a first class ticket to Miami for that Sunday, the twenty-first. I think she went there to tell Connie she was leaving, that she was no longer afraid of her."

We sat in silence for a few minutes then I had to ask, "How is Connie?"

"Dehydrated, suffering from shock. Apparently, she hadn't left her mother's side from the time she died, at least seventy-two hours before we got there. They'll be transferring Connie to Western State Hospital for evaluation as soon as her physical condition is stabilized."

"She...she didn't kill her mother, too, did she?"

"No. The autopsy showed Mrs. Phillips died of a massive heart attack. From what her doctor told us, it wasn't unexpected. She'd suffered several previous minor attacks."

"How did she kill Maureen?"

"We won't know for sure until after the autopsy but it looks like she bashed her head in." He finished the beer and handed me the can. At the door, he gave me a hug. "Don't let it get you down, kid. You did a damned fine job."

I stood on the porch and watched until his tail lights disappeared then went inside. I dictated the final notes on the case, totaled my expenses, made out a bill for Ian, and wrote a refund check for what was left of the retainers he'd given me. Case closed. I should have felt a sense of accomplishment, but I didn't.

The house had never seemed so empty or so lonely. Arthur Trent's needless suicide, Maureen's greed, and Whelan's obsession that had destroyed so many lives, Connie's sickness, the whole case depressed me.

And most of all, Sam's accusations. The fact that he'd said I'd done a good job didn't wipe out the memory of his earlier accusations. In a way he was right. I hadn't taken my work seriously enough. I'd been trying to recreate an image of a hard-boiled private eye based on old movies and books by my favorite authors, books written in the thirties and forties. I was going to have to take a good long look at my life and I wasn't sure I wanted to.

I went into the living room and got out my recorder. Fortunately, the cast left my fingers free. Propping my left arm on the back of a chair, I closed my eyes and began to play *Greensleeves*.

Sometimes music is the only thing that will drive away the dark fuzzies.

Meet the author:

Judith R. Parker makes her home near Ronald, Washington in the central Cascades with her husband, a retired civil engineer, two dogs and six cats. She is a retired corporate CFO.

She has been writing mysteries, suspense and westerns as well as short stories for the past twenty years. Her short stories, some under the pen name, J. R. Parker, have appeared in regional and national magazines and an anthology. Her first book, THE HOUSE SITTER, a suspense novel, was published by Zebra Books in 1994. Her anthology, A KIND OF JUSTICE, was a 2002 EPPIE finalist and her book, RIDE A COLD WIND, won an EPPIE for best western. Two of her books are 2003 EPPIE finalists. Most of her books relate to the northwest.

Parker is a member of Sisters-in-Crime, Women Writing the West, Western Writers of America, Epic, and is a past board member of the Northwest chapter of Mystery Writers of America.

You can visit Judith at
www.inlandnet.com/~judithr

Printed in the United States
42088LVS00001B/124-126